Praise for Lucy Jane Bledsoe

Working Parts

"*Working Parts* is a compelling, amusing, and touching work of fiction." — *Bay Area Reporter*

"*Working Parts* will be a refreshing story for anyone who thrives on stories with complex characters and honest, personal struggle."
— *Philadelphia Gay News*

"[Bledsoe's] mastery of her craft is gracefully evident at every level of *Working Parts*. The book breathes a subtle, yet instantly recognizable, force: that of a skilled writer exerting perfect control over her material." — *Windy City Times*

". . . funny and sad, moving and thoughtful, smoothly written and eminently enjoyable. . ." — *Booklist*

"Anyone looking for a well-written novel with a mix of fascinating characters, both straight and gay, will enjoy *Working Parts*."
— *Lambda Book Report*

Sweat

"Lucy Jane Bledsoe's collection of short fiction is one of the best in recent memory. Her prose is as graceful as her characters and our connection with them as deep as their connections with themselves and each other. Bledsoe is one of the contemporary masters of short fiction." — *Bay Windows*

" . . . it's the intimate, personal moments that resonate most in fiction, like Lucy Jane Bledsoe's story collection *Sweat,* which starts with the tantalizing sentence, 'When I was fifteen I believed that sex was nearly the same thing as softball.'" — *The Advocate*

Working Parts

a novel

———————————

Lucy Jane Bledsoe

Seal Press
Seattle

Seal Press
3131 Western Avenue, Suite 410
Seattle, Washington 98121
sealprss@scn.org

Library of Congress Cataloging-in-Publication Data
Bledsoe, Lucy Jane.
Working parts: a novel / Lucy Jane Bledsoe.
1. Lesbians—Fiction. I. Title.
PS3552.L418W67   1997   813'.54—dc21   96-47425
ISBN 1-878067-94-X

Printed in Canada
10 9 8 7 6 5 4 3 2

Distributed to the trade by Publishers Group West
In Canada: Publishers Group West Canada, Toronto
In Europe and the U.K.: Airlift Book Company, London
In Australia: Banyan Tree Book Company, Kent Town

Cover design by Trina Stahl
Cover photographs provided by © 1996 Photodisc, Inc.
Text design and composition by Rebecca Engrav

ACKNOWLEDGMENTS

Thank you to Linnea Due, Jane Futcher, Ellen McGarrahan and Hilary Mullins for invaluable feedback on drafts. I am also grateful for Holly Morris's smart and sensitive editing, and for the ongoing enthusiasm and hard work of all the women at Seal Press. Most of all, thank you to Patricia Mullan who, besides reading drafts, listens to everything else.

This book could not have been written without the generosity of hundreds of new readers who, over the years, have trusted me with their stories. I am hugely indebted for these gifts.

For my students, newly literate adults,
who have taught me the most
important lessons about language,
reading and writing.

Working Parts

1

I PUSHED OPEN THE LIBRARY DOOR, walked in like I knew what I was doing, then panicked. All those books made me short of breath, a little dizzy. I leaned against the copy machine and willed myself not to turn around and walk out again.

It didn't help that it was September, a time of year that still reminded me of the smell of chalk, erasers, smudgy old textbooks, rain. A time of year that still, though I'd been out of school for ten years, meant confinement, the end of hard play and fruit off the tree.

Besides, libraries were much worse than schools, more condensed. Both places gave me that feeling, like my bowels were made of ice, but at least in school I had some good times too. I loved arguing and laughing in the hallways, hanging out with friends in the lunchroom that always smelled like gravy, and finding a hundred situations a day to finesse. High-school teachers were pushovers. Oh, we definitely had some good times: food fights, torturing substitute teachers, sex in the shop lab with my first boyfriend, long confessional meetings in the girls' bathroom, smoking cigarettes, cutting English. Or Math. Or American History.

School was okay. I graduated, didn't I?

But libraries. They were nothing but books. Lots and lots of books, rows and rows of books. There was something almost arrogant about libraries, or maybe about the books themselves, as if they had some right to whole buildings of their own. Everyone whispered around them as if they deserved all that space.

I was ready to leave. Not even thinking of Mickey's grin, the one that showed he loved me, the one that made me love him, the reason I came in the first place, could keep me here. He'd just have to make his big career move without me because I couldn't do this part.

Then I saw the librarian. She didn't look like any librarians I'd ever seen before. She had ultra-smooth skin, very short black hair and wore big silver earrings with dangling feathers. She stood behind the desk scowling at a huge stapler which lay jacked open on the desktop, her defeated hands resting on top of it. The sight allowed me finally to breathe. Women and machines were my specialties. I waited for her to look up and when she did, I winked. Which got me a big smile.

No way was I going to walk to the back of the library and enter the Literacy Project room with this fine woman watching.

"Can I help you?" she asked.

"Actually, I was going to ask you that," I said, approaching her desk. "Looks like you're having a little trouble with that stapler." I eased it out from under her hands and fiddled with it for about ten seconds, all the time I needed to dislodge the staple jam. I realigned the row of staples, shut the machine and handed it back to her. "Should work now."

She smiled. "What do I owe you?"

She was definitely flirting. And why shouldn't she? I'm not bad-looking. I'm medium height with a cyclist's muscular legs and thin upper body. My shoulder-length brown hair is cut in a wavy shag. I have nice brown eyes, wear squarish-shaped tortoise-shell glasses and have dark skin for a white person. I'm not a knock-out or anything, but I have been told, a few times, that I have very nice breasts.

For a few seconds I enjoyed the encounter with this librarian enough to forget where I was. Her next question brought it all back, hard. "What can I help you find?"

I told myself I could handle it. I started out strong with, "You got any books by . . . ," then stalled out. I couldn't think of a single name. I knew I'd seen authors on Oprah but nothing came to mind. She laughed a little, as if she were nervous for me. Which made me feel grateful to her. Which in turn made me feel indebted to her. Which in yet another turn made me want control over the situation. I felt the first tinglings of a crush. Struggling to finish my sentence, I finally just blurted Mickey's name. " . . . by Mickey Rodriguez. He writes books about bikes."

Smooth, real smooth.

The librarian tapped at a computer. "Mmm. Nothing by that author."

She probably knew I was lying. "Fine," I said. "No problem." I hesitated before leaving, considering asking her out, anything to get some leverage on the feelings of confusion approaching terror that were rocking me. I don't know why I let Mickey talk me into coming here. I don't know why I made an appointment with those people in that back room. I don't know why I thought I was even close to ready for this.

"But let me show you the sports section," the librarian offered. "I'm sure there are a lot of cycling books. Or did you mean *motor*cycle?" A tiny smile tickled the corners of her lips which gave me a dose of courage. My inner butch kicked in. I wanted to say, "Oh yeah baby, I meant *Harleys*," but I only muttered, "No, uh, *cycling* cycling."

I followed her to the opposite side of the library from the one I was supposed to be on. I looked at my watch. Five minutes late. When I spoke to the Literacy Project director, Marilyn, she had made a big deal about punctuality, respecting the tutor's time. I already knew I was supposed to be feeling grateful. I hated being indebted to anyone and I felt indebted already, even before meeting my tutor.

"Yes, here's a whole row of cycling books," the librarian said, leading me down a cramped aisle and gesturing to a high shelf. To steady myself, I concentrated on the fullness in her smile, and in her body. She wore a baggy, thigh-length yellow fuzzy sweater with black stirrup pants. I like big girls in stirrup pants. The skinny ones look too birdlike, but she had these good stocky legs. Her fuzzy sweater just covered her large behind. "Were you looking for bicycle repair books, or . . . ?" Her smile was patient.

"Uh."

"You just want to browse?"

"Thanks," I said and then, after she left, browsed for five minutes so she wouldn't suspect anything. I would pretend I hadn't found what I wanted and just leave. I hated feeling this scared, this out of control, as if I were spinning real fast. Mickey had a lot of nerve pushing me into this. He could take his hundred thousand dollars and start a bike shop by his own crazy self.

Ever since Mickey and I made our deal, after my confession, I'd been hearing my father's voice in my head much more than usual. Now as I stood in this narrow canyon of books I could hear him defend me: *She's too damn smart for school, that's her only problem.* He would toss the report card in the wastepaper basket or tell my mother to ignore the teacher who had asked them to come in for a conference. Then he would put a proud arm around my neck, gently knuckle my head and say, *Reading is for people who are afraid of real living.* After that, we would spend the evening working on our current project: a model airplane, one of those that cost hundreds of dollars and took weeks to complete, or taking apart the blender motor, or a neighbor's car. "Why pay a mechanic?" my father would ask the neighbor. "Lori and I'll fix that for you this weekend." One winter we took apart the gas heater and didn't get it back together for two months. Mom was

6

furious. I didn't blame her. That winter was real cold.

As I made tracks out of the library, I dragged my hand along the backs of the books, proving I wasn't afraid to touch them. I stopped at the door. Suddenly I couldn't move in either direction, out or in. My back started tingling, as if I were being pricked by a thousand tiny needles. Later, months later, I would recognize those prickles as the beginning of authentic desire, a pure feeling of what *I* wanted for *me*, though there would be hundreds of set-backs, false moves and embarrassing returns to adolescent behavior before I came close to recognizing this. At that moment, though, the tingling was enough to turn me around, enough to face me towards the Literacy Project door. Perhaps it wouldn't have been enough to make me suffer the humiliation of walking past that voluptuous librarian on my way to that door, but right then she was nowhere to be seen. "Sorry I'm late," I told Marilyn, sitting down in her small office off the Literacy Project room. A big clock on her desk showed me to be a full fifteen minutes late.

Marilyn smiled a fakey smile, like she was going to let me off this time because it was my first. "Lori, this is your tutor, Deirdre Felix."

I reached out my hand to the other woman sitting in Marilyn's office and barked, "Lori Taylor here. How're ya doin'?" I sounded just like a longshoreman. Mortification bloomed in me like a fever. I undid the buttons at my wrists and at my neck, then realized my undershirt showed and buttoned the top one up again. "Do you have any water?" I wheezed and Marilyn got me a dixie cup of water from the cooler. Somewhere in there I think I heard Deirdre Felix answer, "Fine, thank you. How are you?"

How was I? There were two hot hands around my neck. Cotton stuffed up my nose. My legs ached cold and hot like I had advanced flu. All this made me want to kill someone. Maybe Marilyn. Maybe the tutor.

Deirdre Felix looked like some lady who lived in the hills, a do-gooder come down to the flatlands to help unfortunate illiterates such as myself. Somewhere in her sixties, she had short, wavy gray hair, wore light, tasteful make-up, gray wool slacks, a moss green sweater, probably cashmere, and gold—real, I bet—earrings. Everything about Deirdre Felix seemed one hundred percent, top of the line, the real thing, not a thread of polyester or scrap of plastic in sight.

This would never work. I could tell instantly that I had nothing in common with this lady. As we stood to "get right to work," Deirdre Felix's words, I stopped at the door of Marilyn's office and mustered my best sarcastic look. Her job was to match tutors and students, right? What was she thinking putting me with this Deirdre Felix? Marilyn had swiveled around to face her desk and was already scratching away on a note pad. I knew she knew I was there and purposefully ignored me, refused to turn around and face me. For every second I glared at the back of her head, I wilted a bit, shrunk some, felt younger. I was sixteen in no time.

Mrs. Roach, my sophomore English teacher, was the last one who tried. I remember her sitting me down after class one day. She always wore her thin, straight brown hair pulled back in a loose ponytail and bright red lipstick. She had a passion for Greek mythology and for having the entire class recite the conjunctions. It's the main thing I remember from sophomore English: and, or, for, nor, but, yet, so. She would yell, "Louder!" like we were at a concert singing a refrain and we would all yell out the conjunctions again. On that particular afternoon, her first questions to me were, "Do you eat breakfast? What do you eat?" Then she told me I was smart. Not just smart, she used words like "ingenious" and "an excellent problem-solver" and "witty." She wanted to know what kept me from concentrating in class. I grinned at her like it was a big joke. Mrs. Roach said, "This isn't funny. You won't think this is funny in ten years when you're making a couple dollars an hour flipping hamburgers."

"That'd be fine with me," I smart-mouthed.

"Do you get along with your mom, Lori?"

"Sure."

"Your dad?"

My father had left the previous year. I sat up, looked her in the eye and said, "Yes."

"Do you know that you read at about a third grade level?"

No one had ever put it to me quite like that.

"Books are for people who are afraid of real living," I told Mrs. Roach.

She leveled me one last, mixed-feeling look, like I was a good apple with some bad spots, in danger of rotting through. Then she turned, pulled her chair up to her desk and began grading papers. I stood in the doorway and watched her for a moment, knowing that good intentions, even a kind of warm-heartedness, motivated Mrs. Roach. Deep down, I wanted her to keep trying, but I didn't know how, at sixteen, to walk out of my cage of sarcasm. She never looked up again.

Now standing in another doorway, staring at Marilyn, I felt as trapped by that sarcasm as I had twelve years ago. I forced myself to acknowledge that Marilyn too must be motivated by good intentions, however poorly she did her job in matching learners and tutors. I turned my back, left her office and took a seat in the Literacy Project room with my new tutor.

As Deirdre Felix laid out some paper and pencils, she kept swallowing as if she were nervous. Why was *she* nervous? I glanced at the small pane of glass in the door that led to the library. That librarian goddess could cruise by, look in, and would definitely know which one of us was the tutor and which one the student. I moved my chair to the other side of Deirdre Felix, mumbling something about pressure on a bad leg—I was an expert at instant cover-ups—so that my back was to that window.

"That's some rock on your finger," was my first direct comment to Deirdre Felix. "And I bet it's no rhinestone."

She glanced at her diamond ring, made a little puff sound with her mouth, as if she were dismissing it, and said we should get to know one another a bit. I suggested she start. I learned that Deirdre Felix loved the ballet, was on the board of directors at the art museum, played tennis twice a week and belonged to a reading club.

"What, you sit around and read?"

"Yes."

"Sounds exciting." She didn't respond, so I tried to be polite. "Any kids?"

She sparked up. "My son Jeff is thirty-nine. He's an architect in Seattle."

"Husband?" By the look on her face I guessed I was getting rude again.

"My husband is . . . Arnie. He's a doctor."

That explained the rock on her finger. "Where do you live?"

She hesitated, like I was an ex-convict asking for her specific address, then said, "On Skyline."

"Where on Skyline?" I asked just to make her nervous.

"In Oakland."

I knew that. Skyline ran the length of the crest of the Oakland hills.

"Tell me a little bit about you." She smiled and her lips twitched.

"I work in a bike shop, repairs department. I'm single. Broke up with my last girlfriend a few months ago." An involuntary spasm jerked across her face, but she composed herself quickly, like she met lesbians every day. That's what drives me craziest about liberals. They want you to think that you're no big deal. I'd rather she'd said, "Wow, you're a lesbian. That's weird." Or, "I've never really known a lesbian before." Or even, "Gee, I thought all lesbians were masculine bruisers." Anything honest. Anything other than acting as if I'd just said, "My husband Tom and I have three children."

"What made you want to improve your reading?" she asked.

Later, I'd remember she had used the word "improve," which was generous, even kind, but at the time, I heard only the illiterate meaning behind the sentence. I felt as if she'd slugged me. "You name it, I can fix it," I said, using a line of my father's. "Cars, bikes, toasters, generators, lawn mowers. I'm not dumb."

Deirdre Felix stared at me for a second. "Courage is a form of intelligence," she said. "The fact that you're here proves you're bright. I just meant to ask—"

"Give me a break," I interrupted. "I don't need an inspirational lecture."

The outer corner of her left eye twitched and she took a shallow breath. She picked up her pen and I thought she was going to pack it away in her endangered animal skin purse and leave.

"Sorry," I conceded. "I'm nervous." But I really didn't need people talking heroics to me. I'd seen that TV movie about illiterates, the one with Jane Fonda and Robert DeNiro. This was not a movie. This was real life. Mine.

She didn't leave. Nor did she speak. She raised an eyebrow at me and waited.

My brain cells felt like they were swimming. I tried to concentrate on what to say next, but all I could think was the truth, so that's what I told her. "I'm here because a friend of mine and I made a deal. Mickey's twenty-six and has never kissed anyone. I'm twenty-eight and can't really read. So I'm learning to read and he's finding someone to kiss. It's kind of like a race."

Deirdre Felix smiled. She had great crow's feet at the corners of her eyes, five distinct lines shooting out across each temple. "That's not a very fair deal. Kissing is a lot easier than learning to read."

"Try and tell Mickey that."

"Shall we test your vocabulary?"

The words "test" and "vocabulary" gave me an overwhelming urge to yawn, which I did repeatedly all the way through the rest of our session. Each time I yawned Deirdre Felix gave me a look, which I couldn't quite interpret, but which made me feel like I was using up my allowance of rudeness real fast. An hour later, after I read a couple of passages at about one millionth of a mile per hour with her telling me all the hard words, and after we agreed on a time for meeting again, I was free to leave.

To do so I had to exit the Literacy Project room in full view of the library's front desk and I didn't want that librarian to see me. I could tell her I'd been looking for the bathroom, but for an hour? I could tell her I was a tutor, but even I, bullshitter extraordinaire, didn't feel confident I could pull that one off. I'd just have to wow her with my good looks, obliterate her memory of my coming through that particular door by dazzling her with my entrance.

Okay, that too was a stretch.

I started to slip through the door, sneaking, then forced myself to throw it open boldly, just missing a toddler. I steadied the youngster, or maybe used him to steady myself, then worked at projecting subliminal messages to the librarian, *you want me you want me you want me,* as I strode into the main part of the library. I stopped when I didn't see her. I heard her voice back in the stacks and relieved, left the library unnoticed.

As I got in my car, I felt kind of sad. I'd been sixteen-year-old silly about that librarian and sixteen-year-old rude with the tutor. I can be so obnoxious sometimes. I reminded myself of my father, how he used to get around rich or college-smart people, anyone who thought they were better than him. He would always make sure they knew he wasn't impressed. I wasn't usually like that. I could feel pretty inadequate at times, but I knew better than to let other people see it. My father always made me cringe when he started his peacocking. As a kid I used to promise myself that I'd never be so obvious.

I started the car and decided that next week I'd make an effort to be civil. Deirdre Felix was volunteering her time after all. I guess I had expected her to talk down to me. She seemed to find me annoying, but I sensed that she looked right past the illiterate part of me and got annoyed by me the person. That was nothing new. I annoyed a lot of people. Next time I'd pay attention.

2

"How'd it go?" Mickey asked at work the next day. He was cleaning a chain and had a big smear of grease across his forehead.

"Met a very attractive librarian," I answered, smacking my lips like I'd already tasted her. Mickey and I loved being crude together. "Cruising the library is something I'd never considered."

"Lori," he said sternly. "I'm talking about the reading part."

"Well, aren't we in a humorless mood today."

"Was your tutor nice?" Mickey persisted.

I sucked in my cheeks, crossed my legs, folded my hands, pantomimed hoity-toity to show him Deirdre Felix. I told him about the ballet and the reading club. Mickey laughed, but not much, which made me mad because he was going all serious on this reading thing. "What's wrong with going to the ballet?" he asked. His questions jangled my nerves so I decided to ignore him and started to build a wheel that was supposed to have been ready yesterday.

The cool aluminum in my hands soothed me. I loved the bike

shop, especially the repair room where Mickey and I worked—no, reigned. We considered ourselves the best bike mechanics in town and got away with a lot at the shop because we were so good. I'm not bragging, just stating the facts. Once I tried to tell Mickey how I thought our repair room was the most sensuous place I knew and he looked at me like I was crazy. Mickey is a walks in the rain and candlelight dinners kind of guy. Not me. I'll take machinery over misty sentimentality any day. There's something relievingly carnal about the cold, curved handle of a wrench in my palm, and I loved how that room, full of parts and greasy rags, was completely devoid of façade. There were no tricks there, just tools, means to ends, solutions to problems, hard and cold answers. The floor was just cement, cracked cement, and I loved its stony gray authenticity. No carpet or linoleum tiles to pretend it was something else. I also loved the wooden shelving with varying sizes of compartments that I built my first year at the shop. I kept all the tools and parts so perfectly organized a blind person could have worked there. I even loved the bike grease that found its way onto every surface. Grease is so completely black, so viscous, so useful. Compared to the library, a blurry place built of paper and ideas, my repair room felt essential and comforting.

I was screwing in the new spokes on the wheel rim when Enrique, the shop owner, lumbered in. Enrique and I had a love/ hate thing going. I definitely respected the man. Even if you didn't know how hard he worked or how he'd built the shop from nothing, you knew he was The Man just by looking at him. Well over six feet, he must have weighed a good two hundred and fifty pounds, every bit of it muscle and bone. As far as I could tell he had no social life and not even a hint of a sense of humor. He smiled that Monday morning a few years ago when he came in and saw the wooden shelving I'd built and occasionally when one of us made a great sale, but most of the time he was scowling with concentration. But here was the thing about Enrique: He saw the big picture. As much as he didn't appreciate my work style—I was often late, fooled around a lot and had tendencies toward moodiness—he knew I got the job done and got it done well. In fact, I think Enrique couldn't help himself from liking me even though I drove him crazy. We were kind of like each other's alter egos.

Now he slapped a piece of paper on my work table and one on Mickey's. "Could you read the memo now please. I'd like your feedback." Luckily for me Enrique never really wanted anyone's feedback, that was just a management ploy. As I picked up the piece of paper and pretended to read it, I felt like I had a hummingbird in my chest. I hated that flustery nervous feeling. I'd always had it, but my confession to Mickey and my appointment with Deirdre Felix had turned up the volume on it. After a couple of seconds, I shrugged and handed the memo back to Enrique. Casually I said, "Actually, I don't know. What do *you* think?" A rule of thumb: People love talking and they love giving their own opinions. Even if the question, "What do you think?" doesn't fit the situation, people launch into an answer anyway and forget that they even asked *you* something. By the time Enrique finished blathering on about what he thought, I had a pretty good idea of the contents of the memo. "Sounds good to me," I said good-naturedly.

Enrique hurried out of the repair room again without bothering to ask Mickey what he thought. This happened to Mickey a lot. Because of the way he looked, people treated him like he was retarded or something. I turned to see how he took being overlooked and was caught off-guard by the amazed expression on his face. "I always knew you were a bullshit artist," he said. "But I had no idea you were so good. Don't you ever get caught?"

"Sure, but not often. Then you just say that you don't have your glasses. Or that you have a migraine." I grinned, tried to sound mischievous, but a feeling of shame crawled up my legs.

Mickey gave me one of Mrs. Roach's good-apple-on-the-verge-of-going-bad looks. I hoisted the bike frame up on the stand, tightened the clamp around the down tube and popped on the wheel.

"Man, Lori," Mickey said, still staring. At least he hadn't turned away from me. "How can you do that?" I detected a measure of affection in his voice and wanted to hold onto it for as long as possible, undisturbed, like a warm vapor in the room that would disperse if I spoke, so I didn't answer.

Mickey Rodriguez and I had been friends for five years, for as long as we'd both worked at the bike shop. He thought he was straight, but I told him he couldn't know for sure because, as I'd told Deirdre Felix, he'd had zip for sexual experience. Mickey was in a car accident when he was ten years old. It really tore up his face which now, after the not-so-successful plastic surgery, seemed to be squished all to one side. The way the scars angled down his lips, he looked as if he had two big zippers across his mouth. Even his legs were permanently bent, slightly. He didn't quite limp but being so skinny accentuated the unique angles in his body. I kept thinking he should change his name to Neil or Gary, something real masculine to make up for how vulnerable he looked. He was a great cyclist in spite of his bent legs.

A couple of months ago Mickey told me that he'd gotten sixty-five thousand dollars from the car accident. His parents had invested it for him and now it was more like a hundred thousand. He wanted to open his own bike shop and wanted me to run it with him.

Mickey must have seen the brief "yes" in my eyes. Besides being a good mechanic, I could sell anything. Whenever the people on the floor had a real hard customer, someone who was about to buy but just couldn't make the leap, they'd get me. "Want to talk to one of our mechanics?" they'd ask. "She's an expert. She'll answer your questions more thoroughly than I can." Ten minutes later, the customer would be at the cash register, credit card in hand, often with an upgrade from the bike he or she had been considering. I could sell a high-fat diet to Susan Powter and pornography to Andrea Dworkin. Hell, if given a chance, I could probably sell homosexuality to Newt Gingrich. Mickey and I could make bundles of money. We both knew it.

Before that "yes" reached my lips, though, another set of thoughts bombed my momentary enthusiasm. Enrique was always reading through catalogues, writing up merchandise order forms, taking inventories. He was one of those guys who always had a pencil behind his ear, that's how much writing he did. I could talk fine, knew and used lots of big words, intelligent words, but I didn't like paperwork. Running a business took more than talking skills.

I laughed at Mickey's offer, pretending I thought he was joking, and said, "Are you kidding? I'm definitely not management material." No way. Not me. Never. "I don't want that kind of responsibility. I love repairing bikes." Which was true. I did. I do. I love working parts. A bicycle is the perfect machine. It's gorgeous, even drop-dead gorgeous. I was just happy to have a job that wasn't flipping hamburgers. I liked my life. It was easy. This was cool. I was fine.

Then there was the subterranean reality. I guess you could say that Mickey's offer sparked a crisis for me. I could read the newspaper comics, sure, one word at a time, slowly, like Mrs. Roach said, maybe at a third grade level. I could even make my way through most repair orders. Wheel, paint, chain, cog, spoke, brake cable, these were familiar words to me. I'm not stupid. I catch on quick. I have to. It's sort of like how blind people can smell and hear real well. It's survival. Like if a repair order had me stumped, I'd wait until my hands were totally tied up, or I'd set myself up that way on purpose, then call over to Mickey, "Hey, Mick, take a look at that order on my table? I forgot what I was supposed to be doing. Read it to me, will ya?" Like I'd read it already and just spaced out. There are a million ways to get by. It's not that big of a deal. Like the driver's test. I hustled the guy working the DMV test desk. I told him I'd forgotten my glasses and asked if I could take the test verbally. Then I told him I really liked the gold chains around his neck, cracked some jokes about a couple other DMV employees who I could tell would put you over the edge if you worked there, and got the guy to talk me through the test. I'm telling you, it's easy. There's a way around everything. Like my father, I believed that reading was highly overrated. Voting? I voted for presidents. The rest hardly mattered. Or if there was some big proposition, I heard enough about it to know whether to vote yes or no. I watched a lot of television which, on the eve of the twenty-first century, seemed like a perfectly adequate source of information.

But having our own bike shop. That stopped me in my tracks. I wanted it so bad I had to sit down every time I thought about it. Me and Mickey together. What a dream. For a moment I'd picture myself standing on the floor of a spanking new store, surrounded by gleaming racers and sturdy mountain bikes. A tidy repair room in the back. No Enrique, no boss at all, anywhere in sight. These thoughts brought on much more than that nervous hummingbird feeling, more like an eagle flapping frantically. I wanted that store.

Mickey brought up the idea a couple more times and I always laughed, like he was out of his mind. "Don't even start," I told him the last time he tried to talk to me about it. "The answer is no way, as in no fucking way."

Then Mickey moped for two weeks.

One of the things I love about Mickey is the way his twisted face looks when he smiles or laughs. It's like all the parts have to unfold and rearrange and then there he is all bright and crazy-looking. When he mopes, it's the opposite. His whole face seems to slide even farther to the side. Finally I figured out that he thought I didn't want to go into business with *him*.

Only once had I voluntarily told someone I couldn't read. About a year before I had tried to tell a woman I was dating. She refused to believe me and to prove her point, gave me three thick books for my birthday, commenting that, "If you had some *good* books, you would read." Then she goaded me to read them until I broke up with her.

I didn't want to lose Mickey, though, and I couldn't stand him thinking I was rejecting him. So one evening as we rode our bikes up Spruce Street after work, I said, "Mick, you know it's not that I don't want to have a bike shop with *you,* don't you?"

"I thought we dropped that topic," he said. A beat-up Toyota pickup took a right turn, cutting in front of Mickey, who extended his middle finger at the driver. Flipping off motorists is dangerous—it took Mickey years to break me of the habit—so I knew he was beyond sullen. He was really hurting. Which made me feel like shit.

I waited a second to make sure the Toyota driver wasn't going to circle back and run us down, then said, "I just don't feel like I'd be good at being in charge of something, anything."

Mickey didn't answer. He thought I was making excuses.

I kept trying. "Open your bike shop and I'll work there. I'll be in charge of repairs."

We reached the reservoir at the top of Spruce and headed up Grizzly Peak. If we really moved, we could do the Pinehurst loop and make it back by dark.

Then I got annoyed. "Why are you pouting about this? So what if I don't want to run a bike shop?"

"I don't believe you, that's why," Mickey shouted back to me and picked up our pace. "I know you'd love it. You could sell bikes so fast we couldn't keep them stocked. Besides, you know—and love—bikes down to every last ball bearing. And you do too like being in charge. You love power. So it *is* about me."

I braked so hard my rear tire popped off the pavement, heaving me toward the handlebars. I held on and steadied my bike as the tire bounced down again. I put both feet on the ground. Mickey, still pedaling, turned and looked at me. "What are you doing?" he yelled back.

"Listen to me!" I demanded, then waited for Mickey to turn around and pedal back to me. He stopped, the front tire of his bike touching the front tire of mine like a kiss. The funniest thing about this was that I probably trusted Mickey more than I'd

trusted anyone in my life. Which was pretty funny when you figured he wasn't family, he wasn't a woman, he probably wasn't
even queer. Yet something fell away inside me and I didn't feel
afraid to tell him. "Mick, I can't read. How could I help run a
business?"

"What do you mean you can't read?"

"Paper, words, me—we don't get along."

He blinked a few times and scowled. I could see his mind
working back, trying to think if what I said jived with his experience of me. His thin chest rose and fell as he caught his breath.
"Wow," he finally said and I could tell he believed me. "When did
you—"

He stopped and when he couldn't find the words to go on, I
laughed. "When did I not learn to read? Who knows."

"Are you dyslexic?"

"Oh, I don't know." I hated that word. Teachers had used it
over the years, usually before they ran me through tests. Maybe I
was, maybe I wasn't. My guess was that there were a million reasons I couldn't read, including how no one figured out I needed
glasses until the fourth grade, how much we moved and changed
schools, how my father scoffed at reading, how the goal in school
was to hustle the teacher, not read the books. I had my explana-
tions but they seemed beside the point now, so I stroked the inside curve of my handlebars and said nothing more.

Mickey didn't say anything either but when I looked up, he
had a pleased half-smile on his face. I realized that for Mickey, the
revelation that I couldn't read was secondary to his new under-
standing that I hadn't been rejecting him.

Later, I wished he had rushed in with judgments and denials
and all that stuff most people did because his nutty smile and the
relief in his eyes that our friendship hadn't suffered a break of
trust caused me to make my big mistake. I said, "I guess you kind
of touched a nerve with this bike shop idea. I mean, I sometimes
wonder what it'd be like if I could do anything I wanted. You
know, if I could read. But just thinking about it gives me this

hummingbird feeling in my chest. All panicky."

"Really?" he said thoughtfully. "That's how I feel when I think about kissing a woman."

"Nah!" I barked. "Kissing a woman? Give me a break. That's nothing. Smack, you do it."

Damn, now who was the insensitive one? I sounded just like my ex-girlfriend with her thick books.

"So that's what I say about reading," Mickey snapped. "You open a book and open your eyes. There are the words. Smack, you read. What's the big deal?"

Okay, I'd hurt his feelings and now he'd hurt mine. We were even. "Let's go," I said and took off up the hill, pedaling fast. Suddenly I wanted to get away from Mickey, but he stayed right on my back wheel.

"I'll make you a deal," he called out. "You learn to read and I'll kiss a woman."

"You're crazy," I said.

"No, I'm serious," Mickey yelled.

I tried to ride faster, knowing that I could never ride faster than Mickey, knowing that no matter what, Mickey would always be on my back wheel, right there, riding with me. Which was a scary thought now that he knew everything.

The next day he presented me with the Literacy Project phone number. He even had tried to make an appointment for me but Marilyn told him that the learner, which is what they call the student, had to make the arrangements herself. Just taking that piece of paper from Mr. Busybody Rodriguez made my head feel like it was exploding. I was angry at him the rest of the week and did not call the Literacy Project. I mean, I hadn't handed him the phone number for Overcoming Celibacy, had I?

Three weeks later, after I finally had called the number and had my initial interview with Marilyn, I said to Mickey, "So, kissed anyone lately?" It was sort of cruel but I was still mad at the way he took my reading problem so seriously. It wasn't like he didn't have his own problems to think about.

"No," Mickey said as he accidentally snapped a brake cable, "I haven't."

"Well, you better get going. I'm ahead. I got my first appointment with a tutor."

Mickey didn't even look up. "You're not ahead. I've met someone."

"You have?"

"Yep."

"Deets, boyfriend."

"She's kind of young. I met her at the ice rink."

"What's young?"

"Sixteen."

Sixteen? The ice rink? "Uh, Mickey. What were you doing at the ice rink?"

"Meeting Sheila." He sounded all serious about this sixteen-year-old.

"Well, cool," I said but felt uneasy. I didn't want to think about Mickey being the kind of guy, the kind of *man,* that met young girls at the ice rink. This had to be a phase of some sort, a kind of stepping stone toward his finding an appropriate girlfriend. Or boyfriend. I watched him for a minute as he adjusted the brakes on a Specialized road bike and noticed a new silence in his body, almost like a pause, a space about to be filled.

"Mickey?"

"Yeah."

"Be careful."

3

I DIDN'T GO TO THE SECOND appointment with my tutor. I couldn't see sneaking past that hot librarian week after week. Besides, Deirdre Felix didn't feel right to me. Even if she didn't act too snooty, a doctor's wife who lived in the hills and went to the ballet and art museum just wasn't my type. In a few months I thought I could ask Marilyn for a different tutor. The timing was all wrong. I was busy at work. I didn't have time to practice reading.

"Bullshit," Mickey said. "It's fall. In another month our work will slow way down for the winter. You're not dating anyone. You have lots of time."

"You know Mickey, maybe your own life would have a few more perks if you concentrated on it as hard as you concentrate on mine."

"For someone I always thought of as unusually good-natured, you've gotten pretty testy lately."

"Okay, Freud, next you'll tell me it's my anxiety about learning to read."

Mickey, who was truing a wheel, didn't look up but he raised an eyebrow.

I laughed. "Okay. But if I do go back, it'll be on account of my libido. Remember I told you about that librarian I met at the library?"

"Funny, a librarian in a library."

"Mickey, I'm serious—"

"Lori, you're always turning everything into a sexual tryst. How can you have a crush on someone you met once? I think you're just forcing it on yourself to cover up your feelings about this reading thing."

Mickey could really piss me off sometimes. I didn't even know what "sexual tryst" meant but I bet Mickey had never had one. Where did he get off lecturing me on having too many? I ignored his analysis, refrained from my own comments about his jailbait situation and announced, "Anyway, I'm going to ask her out."

"I can hear your pillow talk now. 'Okay, my little sweetkins, what's this word here? Thaaaaat's right. A little peck on the titty for that one.'"

Mickey loved talking dirty—I figured it was because he hadn't had any—and I never minded. I got right into it. "I'm going, 'Oh, baby, *please.*' 'Uh, uh, uuh. Not until you finish the paragraph.'" Mickey and I were rolling on the cement floor of the repair room holding our stomachs, shouting obscenities and dying laughing, when Enrique waltzed in. Good thing we were good mechanics or we'd have been canned a long time ago.

I didn't tell Mickey I'd signed up for the workshop at the beach. I knew exactly how he'd interpret it: some ratio between my reading problem and sexual obsession. So what if there was a relationship between the two?

Edith, a good friend of mine who'd fallen in love and consequently out of my life a few months ago, talked me into attending Dr. Julie Higginboth's oceanside sex workshop. Edith met her new to-die-for girlfriend at the last one and was sure I'd meet someone just as nourishing. A girlfriend to Edith was like a Powerbar, total sustenance in one compact, bright package. When Edith was in love, I didn't hear from her. I used to get angry, but now I knew that was just Edith. One day the relationship would end and my phone would ring.

The workshop had sounded fun at the time I sent in my check, kind of wild and different, but as I drove to the beach, I cursed Edith. A sex workshop! Besides, how could I trust anyone named Dr. Julie Higginboth? Was she a real doctor? I couldn't find parking anywhere near the beach cabin where the weekend would take place and had to park my car under a sign that said No Parking.

I was a bit late, like an hour, so Doc Julie and the nine other participants were already sitting in a circle on the floor propped up by big womanly pillows. Though it was a bright morning outside, lit candles—tall thin blue ones, short fat white ones, round marbled ones—graced every horizontal surface. Doc Julie asked me to sit down and explained that they were just going over the ground rules for the weekend. I was stricken and Doc Julie knew it. Her eyes said, *I know you're tense now, but you'll be as open and sensual as me by Sunday evening. Just wait.* She reviewed what she had already covered and then said, "Now for the most important rule. I'm going to ask you to form no sexual alliances during the course of these two days. I know this is a weekend on sexuality, but for exactly that reason we must keep trust open throughout the whole group. Of course you're welcome to date one another after this weekend."

This is priceless, I thought. She has just said the number one thing, the magic two words, that will cause a mass orgy: no sex. These women will be doing it in the closets, in the beach grass outside the big window, right on this floor in the middle of the night. Some lucky couple will get caught, maybe right in the middle of their orgasms, be expelled from the weekend and end up staying together for life. Later, the sex doctor will list the couple as one of her successes.

Doc Julie suggested we all hold hands and welcome the Woman Spirit into our circle. As we began our minute of silence, one of the candles started hissing. I wanted to join it. I opened my eyes and stared longingly out the big window at the dazzling sun. I loved autumn at the beach, the harsh contrasts of white sea foam and blue sky, steel cold water and velvet hot sand, fresh breeze and the stench of beached sea life. This pillowy, candle-lit room full of dewy-eyed women made me crave the feel of that pale, dry, scratchy beach grass.

Why had I listened to Edith?

Doc Julie murmured, "Welcome," I supposed to the Woman Spirit.

How can I get out of here?

To begin we were to go around the circle, each woman describing one fear she had about sex. Doc Julie asked the woman two to my right to begin. In the spirit of individuality and rebelliousness, we'd go *counter*clockwise. Good. That gave me seven women before I had to speak. The first woman said she was afraid she wouldn't come. Well, whoopdeedoo. The next woman said she was afraid her partner wouldn't come. She *should* be afraid of that. Then one woman, who was a dead ringer for Barbie, burst into tears and said she was afraid her partner would think she was too fat. I blanked out for the next few confessions, desperately trying to think of what to say. Only three women to go before me.

The woman sitting next to me shifted uncomfortably. I smiled at her and she grimaced back. Her conservative beige chinos with little flaps at the back pockets, pale yellow alligator shirt and brown loafers made her look like an Alice. Or a Maude. Her wispy blond hair brushed against her red-fired face. She looked as if she were about to combust. As her, and also my, turn approached, she eased onto her knees, then stood up. "Excuse me," she whispered and slunk out of the room.

Doc Julie acknowledged the woman's departure with a patronizing smile, hoping, I imagined, that all the other workshop attendees noticed what fear in the extreme looked like. It wasn't pretty. Then, being very egalitarian, as in wanting to be as vulnerable as everyone else in the room even though she was the workshop leader, the doc jumped right in with her own fear. She said she was afraid of peeing during sex, though the way she said it made me think that she was actually proud of peeing during sex, like she thought it might be a turn-on. A feisty woman with fuchsia hair announced that she was afraid of a dildo getting stuck up in her and not being able to get it out because in eighth grade she'd had that experience with a tampon.

I was sure the rest of the women could hear me hyperventilating. What the hell was I going to say? I would kill Edith for getting me into this. There was not one woman here I'd consider touching.

But no one was asking me to touch anyone. Yet. I had to think of a sex fear. What was I afraid of? That after sex the woman would want to move in? That she'd want to file joint tax returns as a political statement? That she'd find out I couldn't read? Damn it, Mickey, for putting this reading thing in the foreground of my mind. Like what did *that* have to do with sex? I guess it had something to do with how I moved on a lot, how I didn't let a woman get to know me, really know me, not like Mickey did.

My mind suddenly slowed way down to that one thought: being found out. Oh, yeah, that did scare me. Shitless. But I wasn't about to talk about being illiterate when everyone else was talking about peeing and stuck dildos. I'm good with bodies. It's the brain part that paralyzes me.

The woman next to me was saying how she was afraid her partner wouldn't understand her need to be touched for a good half hour— *"minimum,"* she emphasized—before she could even think of coming.

Then the room was silent and all nine aroused faces turned toward me. I could hear my breaths come out quivering. I felt a drop of sweat, like a tear, roll down my temple. That did it. I *liked* sex. I didn't need to sit on the floor discussing it with a bunch of strangers. I stood up, which caused everyone to get real still and stare at me. I smiled, said, "Excuse me," loudly, as if I were just going to the bathroom and walked right out the front door.

I knew they all would think I had left because I couldn't handle talking about sex, like I was terrified or amazingly uptight. Maybe I was, maybe I wasn't. I didn't care what they thought. I mean, here was the *ocean*, the womb of earth, a couple hundred yards away, and we were going to sit inside talking about sex fears?

Walking out of the sex workshop felt good, real good. Not rebellious good, which was usually my favorite kind of good feeling, but big and full and rich good, like the ocean. As I walked through the neighborhood streets toward the beach, a stiff breeze blew through my oversized overalls and the air smelled salty and blue. A longing, which I assumed to be lust, flooded my limbs.

Then it occurred to me that maybe the longing wasn't lust. I'd spent a lot of my life thinking about sex—who didn't, right?—but the idea of a *workshop* on sex kind of short-circuited that part of me. I couldn't help thinking about Mickey accusing me of channeling every feeling into something sexual, and he was right, I did. It was kind of shallow of me. Or maybe limiting is the word.

Suddenly I got overwhelmed by a question. This had never happened to me before, the feeling of a question wrapping me like salty wind, washing me like waves. The question was simple. It was about sex or maybe against sex. The question was this: What else is there? There's got to be more. As I thought about my question, a big ache filled my chest, the biggest longing I'd ever felt in my life.

The beach was a short crescent, framed on one end by a cliff and on the other by a rock outcropping. I walked to the cliff, then turned and ran the length of the beach, as fast as I could, trying, I guess, to run past the longing. At the pile of rocks at the other end, I turned and ran back to the cliff. I sprinted the beach three times, finally stopping when I couldn't breathe anymore.

"Hey!" someone called.

I looked up and saw, sitting on the top of a rocky haystack set off from the main rock outcropping, the pale blond woman who'd slunk out of the workshop before me. She had a pad of paper propped on her knee and a pencil in her hand. "Are you okay?"

"Yeah," I said, trying not to pant. "Just running."

A big wave splashed up on the beach, drowning out the beginning of her sentence. "—workshop taking a break?"

"No, I left." I smiled and, still breathing hard, climbed up the rocks until my head was even with her pad of paper. Before she could slap it shut, I saw that she was drawing, not writing.

"Are you an *artiste?*" I asked, pronouncing artist with a fake French accent.

She nodded and I felt stupid for making fun of the word artist. I wished strands of my hair weren't plastered with sweat to my cheeks and neck.

I hoisted myself up and perched my behind on a pointy bit of rock and asked, "Why'd you leave the workshop?"

In the cabin she'd looked too tidy, pink, fragile, but the salt wind roughed up her skin and hair, giving her the look of a seashell, pinky and fine, but also well-traveled and surprisingly resilient. She said, "Oh, I never really meant to come. The weekend was a birthday gift from the women in a business owners networking group I belong to. They meant well. I *am* single, but I don't think this is the way I want to meet women." She looked embarrassed and added, "I mean, nothing's wrong with it. It's just not for me."

"Me neither."

"So then why are you here?"

I lied, "For the same reason, actually. Uh, I mean, my friend Edith signed me up and paid for it and everything. I'm not actually even looking for a girlfriend or anything."

She looked down at her hands.

I fumbled, "I mean, not that you are. I mean—"

"What's your name?" she asked.

"Lori Taylor."

"I'm Whitney Yarbrough."

Scary name. Actually, Whitney Yarbrough was sort of a scary

woman. In spite of the way she had slunk out of the workshop she looked self-assured. She had that I-know-where-I'm-going energy. She was the type of woman who would want to know, right off, what you did for a living.

I checked my fingernails, wishing I'd worked harder at getting all the bicycle grease out from under them.

"What do you do?" she asked.

"Huh?"

"For work."

"Oh. Actually," I bullshitted, succumbing to a sudden need to impress, "that business owners group of yours sounds interesting. I'm actually in the process of opening a bicycle shop actually."

What was that, you dumbo, five actuallies?

And yet bingo, in spite of the actuallies, Whitney's eyes lit up. She touched my arm. "Really! Where is it?"

"Where is what?"

"Your bike shop."

"Oh! Well, uh, my partner, *business* partner that is, and I are just starting actually." Shit! One more actually and I'm out of here. "We have the capital. And we both have a lot of experience in bike retail. We just need the space and you know, to hire our staff and we're off."

"You should join BONG."

I looked blank.

"That's Business Owners Networking Group, the group I was telling you about. It's an all lesbian group, even though the name doesn't exactly reflect that. Kind of closety, I guess." She shrugged apologetically. I couldn't tell if she liked the closety name or not. "They've been a huge help to me. We're mostly small businesses, though, and it sounds like you're going to be a little bigger than small . . ."

She was impressed with me and for a moment it was as if I really did have the bike shop. "What's your business?" I asked.

"I'm a graphic artist. My biggest account is Good Vibrations." She winced, just a tiny bit, but I saw it. "Not exactly my dad's idea

30

of an important account but I'm proud of it. I also have a line of hand-painted greeting cards that are doing pretty well."

"Wow."

She touched my arm again. "Here's my card. The next meeting of BONG is on the twentieth. Give me a call and I'll give you directions. Or," she hesitated, "we could go together. Sometimes it's easier to be personally introduced by a member."

"Okay." I took the card, breathed in the ocean, wondered how much I liked this woman. "Hey, let me see what you were drawing."

When a tender, almost frightened, look crossed her face, I understood. Why would anyone want to bare her creations to anyone else?

Still I insisted. "Just a peak."   She lifted the cover of her sketch pad.

"Gee! Wow! These are beautiful. You shouldn't be shy. These drawings are incredible."

She looked pleased. "They're not drawings, just sketches."

I touched the picture of a swooping bird. When I lifted my finger, I saw that I'd smudged the bird. "Oh no!"

"It's okay. It's just a sketch."

"I'm really sorry." I held up the blackened finger, not wiping it off, as if I could reapply the bird part.

"Don't worry about it." She dropped the cover back down over the sketch.

"You're real talented."

"Thank you," she said and her voice reminded me again of a shell, like I had to put my ear up close to where she opened onto the world to hear her, really hear her.

Whitney stood up, balancing on the jagged rock. "I better go."

"Back to the workshop?"

"No. I'm going home but—" She looked me in the eye and said in an entirely different voice, one that she might have learned in assertiveness training, clear and loud yet lacking solidity, "Give me your phone number."

So I did. She scribbled it on the cover of her sketch pad. "I live in the East Bay too," she said, responding to my area code. "It was nice to meet you." Whitney scrambled down from the rock, then stood in the sand and squinted up at me and the sun.

"Bye," I said, tucking my arms into the bib of my overalls. Later, much later, I'd wish I had asked for the sketch of the swooping bird, that bird that came to represent endangered longing.

"Bye," she said as a foamy wave swept up around her feet, soaking her brown loafers. She laughed, threw her arms in the air and walked away.

After a while I returned to where I'd parked my car, intending to drive home as well, but it was gone. As in towed. I stood still in the place where the car had been, letting the Pacific breeze and hot dry sun buff my skin, feeling too dreamy to get mad. I walked to the police station in town and even took the news that I wouldn't be able to retrieve my car until Monday morning with a floating resignation. I had no choice but to go back to the sex workshop.

I rejoined the group as they were cleaning up after their gourmet vegetarian supper. No one asked me to explain my departure and I didn't offer an explanation. That evening I participated a little bit in the discussions. The ocean and rocks and beach—also some wild purple flowers I had seen blooming in someone's garden and an incredible bird soaring off the cliffs above the beach, the one Whitney had sketched—had triggered something expansive and new in me. As I listened to each woman speak, I listened to *all* of her, not just the words coming out of her mouth, but the way she twisted her hair in her fingers, the openness of her arms as she gestured, the tangle of fear in her eyes, and let her essence drift toward me like a scent. Rather than noticing what was sexy about each of the women, I noticed what was elusive, missing, what I would reach for if I knew her.

That night I left my assigned bed empty and took my sleeping bag out on the back deck. A fog had rolled in from the sea at dusk and now wrapped the house, the deck and me. It shut out the moon and stars and dampened my face as I lay on my back looking into the blackness. A fierce loneliness filled me and for once in my life, I let it. Eventually I slept and in the morning my sleeping bag was soaked.

4

———

THAT WEEK I WENT to the library to see the librarian. My plan was to tell her I had gone to the beach for the weekend, which I had, and wanted a book or two on the California Coast, which I didn't. I figured we'd start talking about the books and I'd ask her out. She looked gorgeous that day in a big sweater as black as her hair, some blue jeans and black lace up boots.

She said, "What a coincidence! I just made a bibliography of California Coast books."

A biblio*what?*

She handed me a sheet of paper. "Look this over. They won't all be in but certainly some will be."

I deliberately had chosen a time I thought the library would be quiet, and I was right, it was quiet, so now she didn't have anything better to do than stand and wait for me.

I glanced over the black ink, then at her black hair, trying to make a connection between what was on this page and something I understood, a woman's beauty. I wondered if her hair were dyed, particularly because her eyes were deep denim blue, but then I noticed her thick black eyebrows, which against her pale skin looked like sideways exclamation marks. If the hair matched the eyebrows, the color must be authentic. I wanted to touch one of those eyebrows. They looked like a brainy person's eyebrows, full with concentration and thought. In high school, even as I was cutting up and making trouble, I always got crushes on the smart girls. Not the quiet, striving ones, but the outlandish, artsy ones, the girls who were smart enough that they could be bad and get away with it.

I looked again at the black ink on the librarian's sheet of paper and finally said, "Look, I'll just go with your best suggestion." I wished my hands weren't shaking.

"It depends on what you want," the librarian pressed. "The bibliography—" I didn't hear the rest of her sentence because just then Deirdre Felix walked out of the Literacy Project office.

My tutor stopped, looked at me and said, "What happened to you last week?"

I had a librarian on one side of me, a tutor on the other, and both were waiting for answers.

I said, "Uh."

Deirdre Felix made that little puff sound with her mouth. *Pfft.* She squeezed my arm and dismissed me, "It's okay." She moved away slowly, like she was really tired, like someone had let her down. Had *I* let her down?

"Wait," I heard myself say. I handed the paper back to the librarian and caught up with Deirdre Felix. When she turned around I noticed that she wore no make-up today and looked older than she had before. She looked like a crumpled tissue. "Were you in there, uh, terminating me?" I flipped my thumb back at Marilyn's office.

"I was getting a new learner." There was a little trail to her voice, like her mind was totally elsewhere. I realized then that I could like Deirdre Felix. I could like her because her tutoring was about her, not about me, not about any other student she might be assigned. I got that same feeling, like curiosity, that I'd had about the women over the weekend. Maybe it was true for all women, that each of us has an elusive quality, a scent of missing something crucial. Deirdre Felix's apparent sorrow, whatever it was about, seemed also to be her strength, at least her strength for me.

Even as I thought all this, I said, "Good," to her news about getting a new learner, as if I was pleased to get off the hook. Then my mouth took on a life of its own and said, "Actually that's not good."

Deirdre Felix still looked preoccupied, like she'd barely heard me.

My mouth pressed on, "Look, I'm sorry about the no-show. I'd like to try again. I will definitely be there next time."

"You were fifteen minutes late the first time. You didn't come the second time. Maybe you're not ready."

"That's two strikes," I said, pleased to have gotten her attention. "You're not out until the third."

"You remind me of Arnie," she said, smiling like it was both pathetic and endearing.

Arnie? Oh yeah, the doctor husband. I was curious. "How so?"

"Always a hustle."

This woman had spent one hour and these few seconds with me. How did she think she knew so much?

She saw how surprised I looked. "I've lived with a hustler for thirty-nine years. I know all the signs."

"I think it's pretty presumptuous of you to think you know me like that," I said feeling bare. I had the old urge to deliver my hardship story—father could never hold down a job, mother giving him the boot when I was fourteen, me going through adolescence without my father, the only person who ever loved me unconditionally. I had the story down, could pour it on like heavy syrup, and it worked, or at least it had worked with most liberal, well-meaning public school teachers and counselors. They were thrilled I'd talk at all. The possibility of my reform gave them hope in their jobs. It was amazing how far you could get on sincerity, faked or otherwise. Sometimes I couldn't tell the difference myself.

As I stood looking at the unimpressed face of this woman who clearly had better things to do than listen to me make excuses, I knew that my stories wouldn't work, just as I had known they wouldn't work on Mrs. Roach. Besides, I finished school ten years ago. This wasn't about hoodwinking teachers anymore. Deirdre Felix looked at me, waiting, while I sweat bullets.

I took a deep breath, paused, glanced at the librarian who seemed busy at her computer, took another breath, then blurted, "I'd just like to learn to read."

The world went absolutely silent. I swear no one on earth moved or spoke in that second. It was as if my fear knifed reality right out of my space. I thought for a moment that I would evaporate. Then I realized that my eyes had filled with tears, which felt like disgrace, bringing reality and noise and my body crashing back down on me. I was here, all right, and so was the rest of this razor-edged world.

"Okay," Deirdre Felix said casually, as if I hadn't just pulled my heart of out my chest and thrown it at her feet, as if I hadn't admitted right out loud that I needed help. "But we start right now. I have an hour. I don't like to waste time. And at strike three, you're out."

"Okay," I croaked, feeling stark naked.

The librarian, who could have overheard everything, continued to stare at her computer screen though she wasn't typing. My whole body had gone cold and trembling and yet I tried to catch her eye before following Deirdre Felix into the Literacy Project room. If I could just wink at her, I'd feel better. She never looked up.

Deirdre Felix and I sat at a table. We had no books, but she produced a pad of paper and asked me to tell her an interesting story about something that had happened to me recently. I should speak slowly so she could write it down and then I would read it back to her, learning to read using my own story.

"Aren't there any beginner books?" I asked. "Don't they give you stuff to work with?"

"We're going to do it this way."

I stared at her. What if I didn't want to do it this way? A welcome jolt of anger invigorated me. "Ooookay," I said, leaning into the anger. Fear is like jelly, but anger is a steel girder. Without something solid to lean against, I'd never get through this hour.

Deirdre Felix, take this. I began, "I broke up with my last girlfriend about four months ago. I'm not interested in being in a relationship right now, I'd just like, uh, to date." I paused so Deirdre Felix could write, congratulated myself for refraining from using the term "fuck buddy," then went on. "So last weekend I went to this beach retreat. It was a workshop. On sexuality." She wanted a story, she would get one. Deirdre Felix puffed her lips and leaned over the pad of paper, waiting with her pen. She didn't look up. "I personally find the idea of a workshop on sex kind of weird, but a friend of mine met her girlfriend that way and she thought I should go." No apologies, I reminded myself. Deirdre Felix was going to get Dr. Julie Higginboth peeing, stuck dildos, the whole shebang.

"So, uh, actually, I wasn't very comfortable the first morning, so I left." I can't believe I just skipped all the good parts! "I don't know, the idea of planning sex, or channeling it somehow, gave my libido the willies. Besides, Mickey told me I think too much about sex and I decided he was right. So I left, just walked out.

"So there I was walking along and feeling really good. It was such a beautiful day and . . . ummm. Uh." My mind blanked out. This wasn't going like it was supposed to go. I was going to tell Deirdre Felix about the sex stuff, not about the ocean and sky and garden and bird.

Deirdre Felix finally looked up from the paper. "Is that the end of your story?"

"No."

I saw her looking at my face, maybe for the first time, and she smiled. Her eyes were the color of warm pewter, a soft and opaque gray. "Well then?" she said.

That beach afternoon flooded my mind and I continued, "As I walked to the beach, I passed by a house with this wild, over-flowing garden. I mean, like it's October, right? Still there were all these flowers blooming. I stood outside the fence for a really long time just staring. There was this one humongous plant with spiky leaves and it had these big fat brushy purple flowers, if you could even call them flowers. They looked like old-fashioned shaving brushes, only much bigger and purple. The whole plant was to-tally ugly and totally beautiful at the same time.

"Then I walked on down to the beach. I met this woman who also ditched the workshop and talked to her for a while. After she left, I sat in the hot sand and looked up at the cliffs. I felt really peaceful, even though there was this big, uh, really huge, craving in my chest."

Why, inquired a dry voice in my head, are you telling this lady, this stranger, all this personal stuff? I felt like the fucking space shuttle: While part of me stayed anchored to earth, another part rocketed into oblivion, totally out of my control. I kept talking.

"As I sat there I watched a bird dive-bombing the shore. Over and over again. Finally it caught something and flew off with the food in its mouth. It was the same bird that Whitney, that woman I met, had been drawing. Or sketching.

"Something about that afternoon, those purple flowers and that diving bird, also that craving feeling, made me know I had to get a grip. Made me *want* to get a grip."

I glanced at Deirdre Felix. With her lips pursed she wrote quickly to keep up. She could be taking dictation from an attor-ney for as impersonal as she looked. "I knew I had to get a grip," I repeated, "like on my life."

Deirdre Felix dotted her *i*'s and put a big black period at the end of the last sentence, as if vision were my problem. She pushed the paper over to me. She had printed neatly. We read my story about five times, working on different words. I felt as if I were chiseling that afternoon into my brain. At the end of our hour, she asked, "What do you want to title this piece?"

"Get a Grip," I said. She made me write that at the top of the page. Talk about feeling like an idiot. There I was grasping the pen hard, like it was alive, a snake with ink in its head, trying to make the letters real neat, like hers. It felt as if I were writing for half an hour. Then she gave me a list of ten words—like *retreat* and *purple* and *libido*—to write over and over again. That was all I had to do, write them.

"Other than that," she said, "I want you to find out what that plant with the purple flowers was. The diving bird too."

I was silent for a moment. That was a lot harder than writing ten words over and over. "What's that got to do with reading?" I asked.

"It's discipline to detail."

What was this, the military? She had to be joking. How was I supposed to find out what those flowers were? Drive back and knock on the door of that beach cabin? And the bird?

I did know that I wasn't supposed to ask this drill sergeant how to do it. I was just supposed to do it.

5

I was disappointed to find out the librarian's name was Pam because I hated that name. It sounded pasty and limp. Yet this Pam was a real firecracker, blazing around the library finding me books on birds and plants while I sat at the table looking through the ones she'd already stacked in front of me. She made what could have been a torturous evening an almost fun one. Maybe it was the contrast of her with the dullness of this room of books, but I could almost see the colors of Pam's aura streaking behind her as she moved about the library. She had lots of energy.

I played it cool, watched her discreetly, smiled little, held back. My crush roared upon me, though, fast and hard. I wanted to gather up her energy, use it myself, relieve her of it, help her expend it. I knew I could make her need me. I could be her resting place, a container to hold her, all of her.

She did have a ravishing body, very complete.

After only an hour, I had found a picture of the bird in a book on coastal birds. I showed Pam the picture. She said, "A peregrine falcon? Wow! You don't see them often." Standing next to me, she leaned down and put her elbows on the table, pouring her breasts over the bottom half of the book, reading about the bird in the top half.

"Peregrine falcon," I repeated, memorizing the words. When she walked off to help someone else, I copied down the letters of the bird's name. It felt kind of good the way my brain drained down into my hand as I formed each letter, like each letter meant something more than itself. I had never gotten that feeling in school, how each of these letters was part of a bird that dove off cliffs to catch fish in the sea. I finished the first word, *peregrine,* and smiled.

Then I wondered if anyone had seen me writing so slowly, seen me gripping the pencil like children grip crayons. I looked up coolly. Pam the librarian was pulling books off the shelf for a bored-looking teenage boy. I tried to relax my hand and let the pencil rest in the crook between my forefinger and thumb, like other adults hold pencils.

As I started to write the second word, *falcon,* I heard two men settling in at the table behind me. They laughed, exchanged inquiries about wives, then quit talking for a moment, shuffling papers, clearing throats. When the low slow rumbling of one man's voice began, I knew instantly what he was doing. I turned and saw the two African-American men sitting side by side at the table. A guy about my age, maybe a little older, like in his thirties, was the one reading, while an elderly man with white hair sat beside him nodding encouragingly. The younger man had his head propped up in his hand as he labored over the words in a children's book. He sounded out each word, letter by letter, going, "Th-eeee, uh, *the.* K-k-k-k aaaa tt, uh, *cat!* The cat—" He leaned back in his chair and laughed out loud, proud of himself for getting "the cat." The tutor clapped him on the back, said, "That's fine, Charles, go on."

A sudden nausea overwhelmed me. In the far corner of the room was another learner/tutor pair I'd been trying to ignore.

The learner was a white woman about fifty years old wearing white-turning-gray stretch pants and a polyester floral print top. She saw me looking at her and smiled. An earnest young woman who looked like she was a student at Cal sat next to her. Why had that woman smiled at me? Had she recognized me as another adult learner?

This program wasn't for me. I wasn't like that white woman in white-turning-gray stretch pants nor like that black man bumbling through his reading, right out loud, right here in the library, like he couldn't care less if the world knew he couldn't read. I wasn't ignorant. I couldn't read too well, but I wasn't totally illiterate.

I forgot all about Pam, pushed back my chair, stood up and left the library.

The day of my next meeting with Deirdre Felix, I called Enrique and told him I had a fever and wouldn't be coming to work. I hadn't written down the word *falcon* and wasn't sure how to spell it. I also hadn't identified that brushy purple flower. Either I finished the assignment or I didn't go to my meeting with Deirdre Felix tonight. I must have made up my mind not to go about twenty times during the day. Strike three, big deal.

And yet, finally, at six o'clock, an hour and a half before my appointment, I returned to the library.

"Hi!" Pam sparked. "You didn't say goodbye the other night."

She looked great in her black miniskirt and red sweater. Miniskirts on big girls are even better than stirrup pants on big girls. I love the guts. It's like she's saying, yeah I'm about a hundred and eighty pounds and I *am* wearing a miniskirt.

"I wanted to look at that book again, the one on coastal birds."

"Which one? You had a lot of books out."

"The one with the falcon."

"Oh! The peregrine falcon! Such cool birds. Hold on, I'll get it."

I sat at the same table and waited for her to bring me the book. As she handed it to me, she winked, dissolving something hard in my belly. Pam in the library was like milk and sugar in bitter tea. After she bustled off, I flipped through the bird pictures until I found mine again. I copied down the letters *f-a-l-c-o-n*.

Then I surveyed the library. The woman in stretch pants wasn't there but Charles was, sitting just one table away. He wore a really nice leather jacket, the kind that feels like butter to the touch, a rich chocolate brown color, and new blue jeans. He was alone this time, reading a children's book again, mouthing the words, holding a finger on each word as he read it, then pushing it on to the next one. His fingers were fine, long and tapered like a musician's. I stared at him, attracted to his leather jacket and hands, repelled by his lack of shame. My gaze finally caused him to look up at me. His eye twitched a couple of times and he rubbed it, then looked down at the book again. He stopped mouthing the words. He turned a couple of pages, looking at the pictures, then shut the book. He glanced at me again before taking the book back to the children's section and shelving it. The most direct route out of the library would have taken him right by my table, but he walked through the bookshelves making a big circle around me to reach the door.

I felt creepy. My discomfort had driven him out of the library, I was sure of it. And yet I was glad he left. I couldn't think with him over there mouthing and fingering words in a children's book.

I looked at the clock. Six-thirty. I went to the rest room, splashed water on my face and got back to work.

Now for the plant. Pam and I looked through a dozen books before we found a picture that matched my plant. It turned out that it wasn't a coastal plant at all, which was why we weren't finding it in the books on coastal plants. It was an artichoke plant gone wild! This really excited Pam the librarian because she thought artichoke plants were spectacular-looking. I assured her that I thought so too, particularly this one that was the size of a small cow and blooming. She couldn't quite believe that an arti-choke plant would be blooming in October but I knew that was the plant I'd seen. "A late-bloomer," I told Pam and gave her my best smile.

I wanted to know what the books said about the peregrine fal-con and artichoke plant, partly because I was interested and partly so I could show Deirdre Felix that I'd done extra. Yet I didn't want to ask Pam to read to me. I didn't know how much she'd over-heard that day in the library with Deirdre Felix, but I preferred to believe she didn't know I was an adult learner. I mean, anyone, even a good reader, trying to identify a plant or a bird would do just what I did, right? You'd study the pictures until you found what you saw. Deirdre Felix had figured that out. She'd thought of a way for me to spend time, a lot of time, in the library with-out embarrassment.

Now I had to find a way to get over to the Literacy Project room. It was seven-thirty-one. By now the library was quiet and Pam had nothing better to do than prop one buttock on my table and flip through the garden vegetables book, making cute, some-times suggestive comments about the plants and vegetables she liked. Her miniskirt hiked up her thigh.

I hadn't seen Deirdre Felix come into the library but that didn't mean she hadn't. I stood up and said, "Be right back."

I walked, as confidently as I could manage, to the back of the library and opened the Literacy Project room door. As I walked through the door, I thought of how Mickey would be proud of the choice I had just made. I'd just exchanged my chances with a hot babe, chances which, by the way, were looking pretty good, for another appointment with my tutor. I tried to feel good about it but virtue never feels as good as it should.

I looked around the empty room, then sat at one of the tables and waited. Seven-thirty-five. A doughy feeling gathered in my stomach. Was I being stood up by my tutor? Was she teaching me a lesson? I was sort of appalled that I cared. I brushed my fingers across the words *peregrine falcon* and *artichoke* written in my notebook. It was no big deal. Just two whole evenings I spent in the library.

Seven-forty, then seven-forty-five.

I did not want to have to talk to or even look at Marilyn, particularly if I was being stood up, but she did work late some nights and I heard rustling in her office. The door was cracked and I peeked in.

"Marilyn?"

"Lori. Hi."

"I had an appointment with Deirdre Felix."

"Didn't she reach you? She called about an hour ago and said she has a cold. She said she would leave a message on your machine."

"Oh!" That was good, that was really good. Not her cold, but that she hadn't stood me up. "I haven't been home."

"Same time next week, she said."

"Thanks."

Pam was humming to herself while shuffling through papers at her desk when I returned to the library. I didn't know what to say so I gathered the coastal bird book and the garden vegetables book off the table where I'd left them and carried them to her desk.

"Can I check these out?"

"Sure. Do you have a card?"

"No." Uh oh. Normally I'd just say forget it but I really wanted those books.

"No problem." She winked again. "Just fill this out and we'll set you up." She pushed a form across the desk at me.

"Sure," I said as the words on the form swirled in my vision. I could write my name and address, but she made me nervous standing there watching. I wrote "Lori Taylor" on the line that said "Name." Then real panic seized me. "You know, I crushed my hand at the shop the other day. It's still real sore. That's why I've been writing real slow." Brilliant, Lori. You're covering all the bases with this one. "Do you mind, I mean since my hand is cramping

46

like crazy, filling this out for me?" I pushed the form back at her and said, "I live on Acton Street . . ."

Bingo. She took the pen right out of my hand and wrote out my library card application. Then she gave me a smile that could only be read as Advanced Teasing. As she stamped the return date on my garden vegetables book, I asked her if she wanted to go see the spectacular artichoke plant at the beach this Saturday.

The flirtation in her eyes wavered. Her hands, which had been lingering on my garden vegetables book even after I took hold of it, retreated to her side of the desk. "I'd love to but I'm busy on Saturday," she said, then smiled again.

So those fiery looks and that bustling enthusiasm was truly for the peregrine falcon and artichoke plant gone wild? No one could be that gaga about books, could they?

I suggested, "How about Sunday?"

Did she hesitate or was that my imagination? "I can't," she said more firmly. "Thank you anyway."

After I was safely out the door, books stuffed under my armpit, I falsettoed, "I can't, thank you anyway."

6
_____

I DROVE STRAIGHT to the ice rink with my two books. I felt
crummy about the rejection from Pam, but not that crummy.
Persistence is the key to successful dating. I enjoyed a challenge
and I'd be back.

Besides I had this crazed feeling about the falcon and artichoke, like they were almost more important than a hot babe in
a miniskirt. What was happening to me? All I knew was that I had
to know everything about that bird and plant. Tonight. I knew
Mickey would read the material to me and I knew he would be at
the ice rink.

A couple of days ago I'd asked him if he wanted to ride after
work. He'd said, "It's going off daylight savings time soon. We
won't be able to ride after work."

"That's no answer, Mickey," I said. "I'm talking about tonight.
There's plenty of light."

He shrugged. "Not to get very far."

"Any ride is better than none."

He was silent.

I got it. He was going to the ice rink. "If you have a date with Sheri—"

"Sheila," he snapped, as if I'd called her a dirty name.

"Sorry. Sheila then. Just say, 'I have a date with Sheila. I can't ride tonight.'"

"Because I don't have a date with Sheila."

"Then come ride with me." I grinned, trying to be my jaunty self, but my grin felt like a jack-o-lantern's, hollow and glowing with only a small flame.

"I'm going skating."

"You're going skating to see Sheila."

"I'm going skating to skate. Sheila may or may not be there."

Romance sure brings out strange things in people's personalities. Edith vaporizes, like it's just too potent for her. But Mickey, I'd never considered how love might affect him. I knew how, in general, he could be a romantic fool, but sneaky and indirect? That had never been his way. He didn't have to lie to me about wanting to be with Sheila. I wasn't going to get in his way. Fine, go to the ice rink, I'd thought that night, I'm perfectly happy riding by myself.

Tonight, though, I needed Mickey.

The ice rink was packed full of young kids and teenagers. Why was Mickey hanging out here? Adult men were supposed to meet women in bars. Or maybe in a biking club. Or even a customer. Mickey could have cruised a customer and talked himself into a date. I should have introduced him to someone, some straight friend, some straight *adult* friend. I didn't like the idea of my best friend hanging out, nightly, at an ice rink.

I crawled up in the bleachers, sat down and watched the skaters, looking for him.

There he was. I had no idea Mickey could skate so well. He held hands with a hefty girl who had lots of dark freckles and short brown hair so tightly curled it seemed to cinch her head. She also skated well. They were flushed, skating fast, their arms swinging in sync. Lots of the other skaters watched them, like they were the main attraction, the act to copy. Mickey spoke to the girl and a moment later their legs, his thin and bent, hers as stocky as tree trunks, instantly changed direction in unison. They were good! I wondered if the girl's parents knew where she was.

The pair skated toward me and I scrambled down the bleachers to the rink side. I arranged my face in a first-meeting kind of smile and called out, "Hey, Mickey!"

They sprayed ice in my face as they skidded to a graceful stop only a few feet away. The girl let go of his hand and he slipped it in his pocket, as if he wanted to protect where she had touched him. Both were solemn, unsmiling, as if skating were holy. I realized that Mickey hadn't heard or seen me, had no idea I was there. A moment later he took off, leaving Sheila balancing on her skate blades, her knees touching, her feet splayed. From where I stood I could see she hadn't a wrinkle on her round delighted face. She pressed her rosy lips together and watched Mickey adoringly as he skated away, made a lovely figure eight turn, then shot back toward her fast, his hair flying out behind him. Another spray of ice and he stopped inches from her, his thin chest almost touching her substantial one. He giggled.

Oh god, I thought, Mickey is in love.

I hugged the two books against my own chest and decided I could wait until the next day to have him read to me. But as I left the ice rink, all my excitement drained away and I knew I wouldn't ask him.

I felt lonely. That same loneliness that took me so powerfully that night at the beach, sleeping in the fog on the deck. A sudden and shocking loneliness. Until recently, lonely had never been a part of my repertoire. Anxious, yes. Terrified, yes. Angry, often. But not lonely.

At home I put a giant tortilla on a plate and grated some

cheddar on it. I chopped up three extra hot jalapeno peppers, which was two more than my usual, and threw them on top, then put the plate in the microwave. When the cheese melted, I rolled up the tortilla and chowed down. The hot cheese seared the roof of my mouth. I wailed and then realized, with the rush of air across my tongue, that the peppers had also lit my entire mouth and throat on fire. I burst into tears and the phone rang.

In spite of my burning mouth, I answered.

"Hello?" I wheezed.

"May I please speak to Lori Taylor?"

"Speaking." I sounded like I had emphysema.

"Lori? This is Whitney Yarbrough. Are you okay?"

"Oh, hi," I said, still choking on my culinary disaster. "I'm fine," I lied. "I just rode my bike fifty miles, so I'm out of breath."

"It's dark out."

"Yeah, I always ride in the dark. With a schedule like mine, it's that or not ride at all." Schedule like mine! I impressed myself, how fast I could become the entrepreneur she thought I was. I opened the freezer, found an old package of hamburger meat, dabbed it against my flaming tongue.

"Oh." Her voice was cool, nearly but not quite businesslike as she said, "BONG is meeting next Thursday night and I wondered if you'd like to come."

"Sure, I'll give it a try," I told her, just wanting to get off the phone and thinking that next Thursday was a long time off and I could always cancel or just not show.

"Why don't I pick you up," Whitney offered. "The group is by invitation only so we like to have new members come with the member who invited them."

Well, it wasn't like I had a brimming social calendar. I didn't even have bike rides with Mickey to look forward to anymore. "Okay."

We said goodbye, I pressed the receiver button, let go and punched Edith's number only to learn that her line had been disconnected and that she could be reached at a new one. Edith must

have moved in her with her girlfriend. Without even telling me.
I hung up without writing down the new number.

7

I LIVED IN A BACKYARD cottage on Acton Street in Berkeley's flatlands. My landlady who lived in the front house was bicoastal, she taught at Cal and her husband lived in Boston where he also taught at a university, so she was hardly ever home. Sometimes when she was out of town I used her barbecue, which she kept on her patio along with two Adirondack chairs. A stubby patch of grass separated the patio from my cottage. There were also fruit trees which produced lots of lemons, plums and apples. My cottage was tiny and expensive, but charming and cozy.

Not that I thought Whitney Yarbrough would be impressed. She probably went for skylights, clean white walls, glass bricks, stark modern art, cactus plants and long bay views.

I put on my green jeans, a long sleeve white T-shirt and a black sweater vest for the BONG meeting. My black cowboy boots were the only shoes I had with a heel and I thought an extra inch or two would be helpful. I wore some biggish silver earrings and fluffed my hair around my shoulders instead of tying it back. Maybe there'd be chemistry between me and some hot babe with a lot of money. Then I could retire and spend my life restoring retro bikes, months searching for rare parts, weeks assembling historically accurate Schwinns, days polishing a single chrome fender . . .

Dream on, girl.

I pulled myself away from the mirror. I knew I should eat before the meeting but food is an ongoing problem for me. I hate cooking and get sick of my usual meals which are one, granola, two, quesadillas, and three, scrambled eggs and toast. In the summer, when my landlady is out of town, I do chicken on the grill. Tonight I was out of granola, tortillas, cheese, eggs and bread, and it was too late, in the evening and the season, for the grill. I considered running out to grab a slice or a food log—cyclist lingo for burrito—but Whitney was due in fifteen minutes.

She arrived five minutes early. At the exact moment she knocked, I noticed the sheet of paper on the floor next to my bed where I'd written my practice words ten times each in clumsy lettering. I felt as if my heart gonged each side of my rib cage once, hard. Get a grip, Lori, I told myself, it's not a dead body. I snatched the paper and shoved it under my bed, then opened the door for Whitney. Her arms were full of apples. "These are all over your yard!" she said. "They're so pretty."

I took one out of her arms and held it up to the light, grateful for something to absorb my attention, calm me. It looked as though it were translucent yellow with swaths of bright red and streaks of bright green. The bunch of them in her arms gave off a scent of sweet tang and earth. Maybe I was just hungry, but I wanted to bury my face in the apples. "Want to come in?"

"Do you use the apples in cooking?" Whitney asked dumping the lot of them in my tiny sink.

"All the time," I joshed, recovering. "I make pies, preserves, dried apples, apple butter, apple strudel."

She laughed and looked around my apartment.

I'm very neat. I may not cook but I do clean. My cottage has two and a half rooms. The bathroom is sizable and has a clawfoot tub. The main room has my four-poster bed and the half-room is a kitchen nook. There's no stove, just a little sink, hot plate and a microwave oven. The main attraction in my cottage is the row of three bicycles hanging from hooks on the ceiling across from the bed. Whitney went right for the one I built myself which was worth about a thousand dollars in parts and would have cost several thousand dollars to buy. She touched a tire respectfully. Her fingers traveled up a spoke and then across the gleaming derailleur. Call me a pervert, but I can't help getting turned on seeing a woman stroke a gorgeous bicycle.

"I have a Bianchi," she said.

"Mmm," I said.

She turned fast. "You don't like Bianchis?"

"I didn't say that."

"But you sounded like you don't like them."

"Some people like them. It's all about fit." I didn't add that I didn't know anyone who fit a Bianchi, that in my experience they're bikes for people who don't know bikes and want to ride a label. Kind of like driving an Audi, quasi-classy but definitely not the real thing.

"Ready?" I asked to change the subject.

She nodded. Whitney wore double-pleated gray trousers and a pink cotton sweater. Her earrings were little brass cats. For a fast second I imagined my date was Pam, big, brimming, mini-skirted Pam, and the fantasy shook me hard, weakened my joints.

"I like your place," Whitney said as I locked the door. She tapped her finger against a rose thorn. "This climbing rose is huge. It practically covers your whole house. Does it bloom?"

"Oh yeah. Yellow. It's spectacular in the summer."

"I'd like to see it," she said following me down the path to the street, "in bloom."

Her voice was casual, a comment just tossed off, and yet it was tossed into the future, tossed *months* in the future, like a wish.

～

During wine and puff pastry hors d'oeuvres, of which I'd eaten about twenty within the first half hour, Whitney introduced me to a lot of friendly women. I noticed that they were all white and all sparking with apparent good health. The house, which was near the top of Spruce Street in the Berkeley hills, had skylights, clean white walls, glass bricks and long bay views, though I didn't see any stark modern art or cactus plants. The whole place smelled like gardenias.

"What are these?" I asked the hostess, a curly-headed woman named Alix, as I started to touch a long green stalk with a deep red neck, an orange crest, and a purple spike, like a unicorn's horn. Five of these stalks were arranged in a vase of thick purple glass. I thought better of touching anything and withdrew my hand.

"Oh touch them!" Alix laughed shaking her long brown curls. "Birds of paradise. Aren't they lovely?"

They were. I wondered if Deirdre Felix knew about birds of paradise. At my appointment with her last week, after I showed her the names of the bird and plant, she told me that she had a garden and loved plants. Better than animals, she had said. Plants were more remarkable because they made their own food from sunlight whereas animals were dependent and greedy by nature. We're animals, of course, she had added, so naturally we're endeared to them. But they aren't as good as plants.

This had been the most she'd ever said to me and the closest by far to revealing anything personal. I think she surprised herself because she snapped right back into her businesslike manner. Not before a warm curiosity, though, like a long stretch, pulled through me. This week I would ask her whether she grew birds of paradise in her garden.

"This is Joy, my best friend from Oberlin," Whitney said holding the hand of a woman who had red cheeks, dark bangs and a long dark braid down her back.

I turned away from the birds of paradise, smiled politely and asked, "Where's that?"

"Oberlin," Whitney prompted.

"Is that where you lived before here?"

A moment of silence told me that I'd said something dumb.

Joy said, "Oberlin College. We were roommates our senior year."

"Oh! Oberlin!" I chuckled, as if to excuse a silly lapse. "You didn't tell me you went to Oberlin. I'm getting some more wine, can I get you some?"

Simultaneously Whitney asked, as I knew she would, "Where'd you go to college?"

I wrested the wineglass out of her hand, though it was still a third full, smiled my most flirtatious smile at Whitney's best friend from Oberlin and made a beeline for the chow table without answering.

As I filled the two wineglasses embarrassingly full and stuffed several more puff pastry tidbits into my mouth, an impulse so strong, so visceral, overwhelmed me that I had to set down the wineglasses. I wanted something in my hands, something I could fix, something with cold hard parts that fit together with perfect little "clink" or "pop" sounds. I thought about my dad, missed him, wondered if I should call him tonight, wondered if the number I had was still good. Most times it wasn't.

"Are you okay?" Whitney was at my side.

"Just shy," I said, handing her one brimming wineglass.

"Come on, we're starting the meeting." She tucked a hand in my elbow and pulled me to the white leather couch. The couch smelled like raw cow—it must have been new—and made that expensive squeaking leather sound as I sat down. A splash of wine washed out of the glass and onto my lap.

Alix began the meeting by reading a poem on achieving your dreams and then the members of BONG took turns sharing their business-related trials and successes since the last meeting a month ago. Whitney, it turned out, had a lot to report. "It's been an incredible month for me," she said. "I got two new big accounts." Several women cheered and clapped. She smiled and continued, "The first is Garden Variety, a New Age yard and garden store."

"Ooooh!" Most of the group cooed. "*Fab*ulous."

"And I'll be doing all the ads and catalogues for Sweet Tooth, that candy store on Castro. Also, four new stores have picked up my greeting cards."

"Whitney, that's so great!" I said genuinely impressed. She was such a good artist, I knew she deserved this success. Her tentative grin made me bolder and I patted, then squeezed, her knee.

"I'm a little nervous about the cards," she added. "These are my naked women ones. My dad'll just choke." She laughed dryly and I could tell she didn't think it was funny at all.

A very tall woman with a short silver spiked haircut said, "You're getting there, Whitney. Before long you'll have a real business."

I felt Whitney slump a little. She was so susceptible to anything that smelled like criticism. I butted her gently with my shoulder and when she looked at me, winked.

"What you need to do now," the silver-haired woman advised, "is keep the ball rolling. These two new accounts can help you get others." Her tone suggested Whitney would never pull it off.

I chimed in, "Whitney's ball seems to be rolling pretty good already."

I think I detected a snicker from Joy who then asked the silver-haired woman, "How's your copy store, Dory?"

I whispered in Whitney's ear, "Dory's jealous. Congratulations on your new accounts."

Whitney didn't answer or even look at me, but she blushed.

Dory reported a long roster of accomplishments for the month, mentioned no setbacks and offered advice to several more of the women who'd spoken before her. By the time she finished talking I knew that her business made about five million times more money than anyone else's and that she believed that gave her the right, even the obligation, to lecture.

"A copy store," I said when she finally shut up. "Now that's smart. How could you possibly go wrong with a copy store? Easy money."

My comment inspired an unnatural silence. Okay, so I'd put in a little dig, but someone had to say it. There's a big difference between trying to make it as an artist and owning a copy store. Whitney could be raking it in, too, if she weren't doing something she felt passionate about.

Alix the hostess shook her brown curls, as if to clear the air, and suggested a closing ritual. Before I found out what that was, Dory interrupted her and said, "What about our new member? We haven't heard from her yet."

They all looked at me.

"Whitney says you're starting a business," Dory prompted.

"Uh, yeah."

"Tell us about it!" Joy from Oberlin enthused.

"Yeah, well, uh, my friend Mickey and I are starting it together. A bike shop." They waited and I knew I had to supply details, wing it big time. "We figure we need about two thousand square feet."

"Big!" someone exuded.

"Hmm, ambitious," Dory forewarned failure.

I looked her in the eye and my bullshit expertise kicked in. "That's right. Why start small, huh? When you know you have a good idea, you have to go with it. Mickey and I figure we'll run the shop ourselves the first year. We'll be working our butts off, but we get along real well and we both like to work."

Dory harrumphed, "Just wait until the honeymoon is over."

I continued over her voice, "I want to stock nice bikes for beginning riders as well as some higher end gear for serious cyclists. I want to be a really welcoming shop, not snotty like some of the places in town. Our dream is to eventually have a shop club, not for racers, but for serious recreational riders." Every single word that came out of my mouth was news to me. I made it up as I went but it sounded pretty good.

"What about capital?" Dory drilled.

"Got it."

Her eyebrows went up. Though she sat all the way across the room, I felt her shift, sidle up to me. I could tell Dory was a woman who warmed to the word "capital" especially when followed by the words "Got it."

"Have you started looking for space?" Joy asked.

"Yes," I lied. "Haven't found anything yet."

"Do you plan to open with full or partial inventory?"

A moment of panic, then I blazed forward, "Full, definitely."

They pitched question after question at me and I slugged each one out of the ballpark. My confidence soared and so did their admiration. Dory started biting her nails.

"What you need," Joy pushed forward and perched on the edge of her chair, "is to build your customer base fast to support the large inventory and rent. Let's brainstorm for a minute on how she could do that." Unlike Dory's, her advice came from excitement and support. It felt good.

Ideas flowed out of the women. You'd think selling bikes was their primary mission in life.

Whitney handed me a note pad and a pen. "You may want to write some of these ideas down," she suggested.

"Oh no thanks," I said, pushing away the note pad and pen. My exhilaration burst and flattened. The room went quiet again, and I realized that I had sounded disdainful, like I wouldn't be interested in any of their ideas. "I have a very excellent memory actually. I remember everything. Actually I listen best when I don't write at all. When I just listen actually."

Shit, the *actuallies* were back. And now I sounded like I'd just said I was brilliant, like I had a photographic memory or something. The women shifted in their chairs, twisted buttons, cleared throats, then I guess they decided I was okay, that I wasn't as arrogant as I sounded, because the avalanche of support gushed forth again.

It did feel good. I was touched by their excitement and willingness to give me ideas, but soon their genuineness made me feel guilty about being a fraud. Some day, like six months from now, long after I'd quit coming to these meetings, someone would say, "What happened to that woman who was going to start a bike shop?"

"She sounded so together," someone would comment.

Dory would snort once to say she knew all along that I'd never open any bike shop.

I looked around the circle of women, their hands gesturing, their bodies bobbing, their eyes sparking, all for me. They certainly were zealous, these healthy gang-buster entrepreneurs, but I could no longer hear what they were saying. I'd created this enthusiasm and wouldn't be able to back it up. I felt the kind of panic I used to feel in my drug-taking days, as the drug wore off and there was just me sitting there.

For a few minutes I had had a bike shop, a wildly successful one.

It was late when Whitney dropped me off at home. We'd been the two stars of the meeting, with her new successes and my brilliant plans. "Congratulations again," I said, getting out of the car. "I know who to come to for my bike shop ads."

She smiled, didn't say anything and looked at me too intently. I hoped that didn't mean she wanted to be invited in. The contrasts in Whitney Yarbrough scared me. She was pink and gray, tender and rock hard. She triggered my rescue fantasies—when her confidence flagged, when she worried about her father's opinions—and at the same time made me feel inadequate. In spite of her flagging confidence, she would in fact succeed at anything she tried to do and expected the same of others, of me. I could see myself trying to save her and scrambling to impress her at the same time, a combination that would tie me in knots.

I vowed to make better efforts to get Pam to date me. She had to. I could devote myself to a woman who, like her, was already full.

"Thanks for taking me." I slammed the door a little too hard.

8

_____

"I'D LOVE TO BUT I'M BUSY that night," I told Whitney when she called a week later to ask if I'd like to go see San Francisco's new art museum.

I didn't lie. I had my fifth meeting with Deirdre Felix that night. However, I did not add that I'd like to do it another night. I admired Whitney—I'd even gone to the bookstore to buy a few of her greeting cards, minimal line drawings of women's bodies accented with washes of water color, and they were so pretty I propped them up on the windowsill in my bathroom—but admiration is not enough. Thoughts of Whitney did not comfort me the way thoughts of big, overdressed, take-life-by-the-horns Pam did. Pam was a challenge, a handful, no, more like a bodyful, and she was who my pillow became at night.

It rained all of November. I spent my evenings watching television, wondering if I should call Edith at her new number, listening to Mickey's post-skating, late-night odes to Sheila—he was definitely in love—and late-late-night soaking in my clawfoot tub, looking at my flash cards.

"Sorry about these," Deirdre Felix had said. "Flash cards remind me of grade school and I bet they do you too. But they really are the best way to learn new words. You just have to review them over and over again, that's all there is to it."

The flash cards did remind me of grade school and I did hate them, but having her admit how awful they were made it harder for me to rebel. I was supposed to review them nightly and I always put it off until the very end of the evening. Sometimes I fell asleep with them in bed and dreamt of giant *e*'s and *s*'s floating in space, like ideas that I just couldn't grasp.

These flash cards, the feeling of a pen in my hand, just the sight of lined paper and Deirdre Felix herself, especially Deirdre Felix herself, inspired such a wilderness of feeling in me. Forceful and tangled, I couldn't even tell if the feelings were positive or negative, if I hated or loved Deirdre Felix. I felt myself becoming attached, that much I knew, but sometimes it felt like an attachment of fury, like she was the conduit to my becoming a maniac of some sort. I could go from the tenderest thoughts, like trying to imagine what position she slept in at night, to visions of taking a machete to her garden, all in about ten seconds. Every single week I was positive I would quit, would not go to my appointment, then at the last second, would go.

One afternoon late in the month of November, I laid on my bed after a cold wet ride on my mountain bike followed by a long hot soak in my clawfoot tub and tried to study the flash cards. I had an appointment with Deirdre Felix in an hour.

Looking at the cards one at a time, each with its string of letters like little black spiders, made me restless. When I felt that way, that scraping feeling along my spine, Deirdre Felix said to try touching the letters, to trace my finger along the lines. I placed my middle finger, the fuck you finger, on the first letter of the word *endurance* and began to trace the *e*.

Then I hurled the whole stack of flash cards across the room. They fluttered like pigeons and came to rest on the rug and kitchenette floor, some with the words turned up and others with the words turned down. I narrowed my eyes at the flash cards, threatening them, wanting to get up and turn the word-up ones the other way so I didn't have to see them at all. I hated them. I hated every single word Deirdre Felix ever had written on a card. Trying to learn those words felt like putting my head in a pencil sharpener, making me focus my thinking down to a piercing point.

I closed my eyes and thought of big soft Pam on top of me, smothering that needle-brain feeling with hot liquid pleasure. I imagined her mouth on my neck, her hands tracing my ribs. Her buttocks were like those of the women Whitney drew, full moons, enough flesh to fill a heart, to flush out a brain. I wondered how she liked to be made love to, then challenged myself to think of ten radically different ways to make her come. I'd gotten to number eight, which was real kinky and even difficult physically, when the siren of a police car tearing by on the street outside sliced open my fantasy. I laid there too raw, too overstimulated to move. Pam wasn't here. Why wasn't she? Why was I alone? Why for two months had she flirted mercilessly and yet refused to go out with me? I had asked her at least four times.

I rolled my head to the side and looked at my bedside clock. I had thirty minutes to make it to my appointment with Deirdre Felix. That excited feeling I had a month ago when I found the peregrine falcon and artichoke plant felt like a hologram. It was there, I could see it, but I couldn't touch it.

What was the point really? It wasn't like at my age I was going to learn to read well enough to make a difference. Nothing would change if I learned a handful of words. I was never going to sit around reading fat novels and I'd buy a car the same way I did the last time. The guy at the bank pushed a document covered with print as dense as swarming ants across the desk at me. I ran my eyes over the five pages, pretended I was reading them and signed. When I took the loan papers home, I sat down and tried to read them for real. I got through one sentence and felt like someone was holding a pillow over my face. I'd never be able to read that shit, no matter how many years Deirdre Felix drilled me with her flash cards. If I just laid here on my bed where it was warm and dry I would miss my appointment and that would be the end of it.

Then I wondered what Pam was wearing today.

I heaved myself off the bed and still vibrating with sexual tension, pulled on fresh jeans and an oversized kiwi-colored sweatshirt. I washed my glasses, brushed my hair and decided to walk the eight blocks to the library. It was only misting after all, not really raining.

Two blocks from home, it began pouring. By the time I reached the library, my hair and jacket were soaked. I shook my head like a dog before entering the building. Pam stood at the front counter, just hanging up the phone.

"How're ya doing?" I asked, leaning on the counter.

"Good. You?"

"Great, except for being a little wet."

"It's that kind of day." She offered one of her flirty smiles, propped her elbows on the counter, leaned toward me. I wanted to reach up and stroke one of those black eyebrows.

"Yeah," I agreed, perversely trying to make her comment suggestive. I opened my mouth to propose a movie later on, but she laid a hand on my wrist, said, "Just a second" and turned to answer a coworker who called her from the back room. I heard a tiny hiss, like the sound of air leaking out of a tire, coming from where her hand touched my wrist. As she conducted her business with the coworker, I indulged my eyes. She looked a bit different. Maybe she'd gained some weight, her face was sort of puffy. Her skin too was changed, brighter somehow. It was almost glowing, like it was lit from behind. I tried to believe I'd put that glow there and the thought gave me confidence. When she turned back to me, I put my fingers over hers, keeping her hand on my wrist, and said, "Look, Pam. I'd really like to see you outside of the library some time. How about catching a movie—"

"Hi," said a boisterous voice right in my ear.

Standing in my space, like about six inches from my shoulder, was the fiftyish-year-old adult learner who I'd seen my first night in the library and many times since. Most Wednesday nights she was in the Literacy Project room working with her tutor at the same time I worked with mine.

She bellowed, "I see you every week but we've never met. I'm Lillian!"

I ignored her outstretched hand, tried to look as if I'd never seen her in my life and said coldly, "I'm Lori."

"Nice to meet you! See you in there!" Lillian headed cheerfully for the Literacy Project door.

I gave Pam a look and shrugged, as if I had no idea who the woman was, as if she were crazy, then said, "I gotta run," forgetting that I was in the middle of asking her out.

I did not follow Lillian to the Literacy Project room, where I knew that Deirdre Felix, who always seemed to arrive early, sat checking her watch every ten seconds, waiting for me. Instead I left the library. I couldn't bear another hour-long session of exposure, of feeling like a total imbecile. I wasn't like that jolly woman in polyester, or any of the other people in the program. I just couldn't do this. I didn't want to let Deirdre Felix down, I really didn't, but all I wanted was Pam all over my face, it was all I could think about right then, or more to the point, all that I could feel because sex wasn't thinking and that was a big relief.

I repeatedly slammed my palm against the wet side of the cinder block library building, saying "shit" with each slap, as I headed down the sidewalk in the rain. University Avenue was clogged with honking, screeching traffic, as if the drivers thought making noise would improve the weather. I'd only gone about ten yards when I heard a long honk followed by screaming brakes. I turned to watch a new tan BMW hold up traffic as it tried to back into a parking space in front of the library. The car behind it, the one that had braked so hard, crept forward, crowding the BMW so that it could not get into the parking space.

I watched the two cars battle it out under the blinking green-ish light of a defective street lamp. The BMW inched back, the car behind it inched forward, until their bumpers touched. More honking, then finally a small woman wearing nothing but a white tennis skirt, a pastel tennis top and no jacket jumped out of the passenger side of the BMW into the blinking greenish light and pouring rain. It was Deirdre Felix.

She landed in the stream of rainwater gushing down University Avenue along the curb, soaking her white tennis shoes. Where was the '67 Saab she usually drove? She yanked open the back door of the Beamer, reached in and pulled out a big canvas bag and a tennis racquet. Then, with her head and shoulders still in the car, she brandished the tennis racquet in the air behind her as she shouted at the driver whom I couldn't see. I couldn't make out her words but the tone was enraged, high-pitched and final. She finished with one big self-contained sob, then pulled out and slammed the door. Whoever was driving the Beamer wasted no time shooting back into the traffic, causing more honking and braking. Deirdre Felix tucked her head and charged through the rain toward the library entrance.

Though I couldn't help feeling pleased that I'd caught Deirdre Felix arriving fifteen minutes late, I hated seeing her so defense-less—wearing hardly any clothes and clearly traumatized by that BMW driver—all in pouring rain.

And I had thought her life was seamless!

I hurried back into the library, walked right past Pam and went back to the Literacy Project room. Deirdre Felix wasn't there yet. I guessed she'd stopped in the rest room. I slid into a chair at a desk, my back to Lillian and her tutor who sat at a table across the room, and tried to look as if I'd been waiting fifteen minutes. I lifted my wrist, looked at my watch and held that pose until Deirdre Felix trotted in, wild-eyed and wet.

She didn't even say hello as she pulled out a chair, thunked down her big bag, unzipped it and pulled out a tablet, pens and the sailing book. Rainwater streamed from her head onto the tablet and she said, "Damn."

"Are you okay?" I asked. "Where's your jacket?" I didn't want to let on that I'd seen her screaming at the Beamer driver.

"*Pfft*," she said, as if showing up in soaking wet tennis togs was normal. "I'm fine. It's a long story but it wasn't raining when I left the house this morning for tennis and I expected to be going home long before coming here. I'm sorry I'm late."

"I guess that's strike one for you, huh?"

I meant it as a joke, kind of to lighten things up a little, but she didn't take it that way. She sat up straighter and looked at me. A little streak of mascara smeared down the outside of her eye like a black tear. "That's right," she said solemnly with a hint of anger, "strike one." She picked up a pen and crossed her bare legs. One had blue raised varicose veins running down the outside, both had cellulite on the thighs.

"Don't you want to dry off or something?" I said carefully, sorry I'd angered her. "I could get you some tea. I think Marilyn has hot water in her office."

"No. I'm fine. Let's begin." She opened the sailing book we'd been reading the last couple of weeks. I was still only part way through chapter one. The sight of all that print reminded me that I'd been on my way out of the library, out of the program for good, only a few minutes ago. Why did the sight of Deirdre Felix in distress have to draw me back?

I glanced across the room at Lillian who was still talking and laughing loudly with her tutor. Every week I listened to her procrastinate by telling long stories about her grandchildren, and her tutor let her.

I put my finger on the first word in the paragraph where I'd left off last week, thought of Charles and withdrew it, then started reading. Deirdre Felix's stomach growled twice as I battled the paragraph.

Lillian babbled on.

My finger strayed back to the page. I yanked it away.

I heard Pam's voice right outside the Literacy Project door.

Deirdre Felix's stomach growled again.

I'd read about ten words and hadn't a clue what they were or what they meant.

I put my finger on the next word and tried to concentrate.

I thought of how Whitney had tapped the rose thorn with her finger. I thought of putting my finger on Pam's center of being.

Deirdre Felix's stomach growled and Lillian *still* jabbered about her grandchildren.

I looked at my finger touching the word. I thought of Charles pushing his finger along. I thought of Whitney's finger on the spokes of my handmade racer.

"This is dumb," I announced, pushing the book away from me like a plate of bad food. Why hadn't I just walked home in the rain! Why had I come running in here after a soaking wet lady in tennis togs?

Deirdre Felix wiped her eye, smearing more mascara across her temple. She asked, "What's dumb about it? You said you liked adventure stories."

Her voice was dull, a monotone, like she was just putting in the hour she'd signed up for, her obligation.

I said, "It's about a man, for one. Boy this, boy that, conquer this, conquer that. If a woman were telling this story, it'd be totally different."

She stared at me.

"Secondly, sailing doesn't interest me."

"Well."

"Third off, you've obviously had a bad day, this is obviously a totally inconvenient time for you. Why'd you bother to come? I mean, I'm not going to be hurt if you don't show, you know."

I hated my tone. I wanted to be kind. I wanted to be the one fixing something for *her*, not her the one that was supposed to fix something for me. But that wasn't the deal. I was the fixee, she was the fixer and I hated it. I wanted to make her a cup of tea or find her a warm sweater, anything sensible, anything other than the ludicrousness of two soaking wet women sitting at a table pretending that one was teaching the other to read.

Deirdre Felix wiped her hand across the damp tablet once, then closed the sailing book and looked at the cover which pictured a hunky white guy hanging off the side of a small sailboat, a big wave splashing over him. I ran my fingers through my wet hair. She ran her fingers through her wet hair. She looked so sad. Old too.

She said, "Why don't you tell me another story. I'll write it down and—"

"I'm tired of that. We've done that three times."

I felt so confused. Between wanting Pam, fearing Lillian, feeling I-don't-know-what for Deirdre Felix, I was choking on an emotional hairball. I didn't want to start acting adolescent again but felt my inner teenager getting ready to attack. I guess Deirdre Felix saw it too because she leaned back and shook her head.

"Oh, Lori," she said. The little pockets of tension all over her face let go. Everything sagged a bit.

"What?" I asked. "What?"

For a brief moment, a very tiny moment, the thought occurred to me that maybe she did need me, that for whatever reasons she really did want to be here. But then she said, "You're right. This isn't a good time for me. Do you mind? Next week?"

She packed her canvas bag and left. I wished I had said something about hoping the week got better for her.

I sat and listened to Lillian finally working on her lesson until it occurred to me to wonder how Deirdre Felix was going to get home. I jumped up and rushed through the library, again ignoring Pam, and out to the street. Deirdre Felix stood at the bus stop, down the block at the corner of University and San Pablo, in the pouring rain, wearing only her mint green and white tennis togs, her legs and arms bare. She looked small and defenseless, like a street person caught in the storm, not like a doctor's wife who had a big house in the hills.

I realized I had walked to the library, didn't have my car, but could offer her my jacket. As I stripped it off and ran down to the bus stop, a bus pulled up, farting black carbon monoxide into the wet air, and Deirdre Felix climbed on board. I arrived in time to see her, through the rain-streaked bus window, fall into a seat close to the driver. She looked out the window. I smiled and held up my jacket, gesturing at it with my other hand. She didn't smile, but shook her head and fluttered her fingers in what I guessed was a little wave. The bus pulled from the curb, away from me, and lumbered down toward the marina. I knew that wasn't the right bus. I knew that she couldn't possibly get to her home on Skyline Boulevard by riding that bus.

Standing in the dark, in the rain, watching Deirdre Felix be carried off by a big old dirty bus headed in the wrong direction, I was struck by an intensely lucid feeling. It was as if the fabric of the world tore apart and I could see through to the feelings of the things rather than just the picture fronts of the things. The world felt extremely slick, as if friction had disappeared altogether, as if I had gotten on a very fast ride and wouldn't be let off for a long, long time.

Deirdre Felix, I was sure, was on the ride with me.

9

THE NEXT WEEK, on the first Wednesday in December, Deirdre Felix showed up wearing gray flannel slacks, a red wool blazer and a London Fog raincoat, looking composed and elegant, as if her disheveled state and flight by bus the previous week had been a figment of my imagination. She didn't mention my appearance at the bus window or my offer of my jacket and somehow it was as if it all never had happened.

"You know you're right about that sailing book," she said right off. "It would be a much different story if a woman wrote it. That guy wasn't very interested in his experiences, only his accomplishments. It put me in mind of your peregrine falcon and artichoke plant. That guy would never have noticed such marvelous details."

My insides flushed hot. Was that a compliment?

Then she told me her tape recorder idea. She wanted me to keep a journal on tape. I was supposed to talk into the machine for five minutes every day.

I realized that the compliment about "marvelous details" had been a setup.

"What does talking have to do with reading?" I asked.

"It's discipline to detail."

"What do you mean?"

She didn't answer. She shuffled through the flash cards with my vocabulary words on them, then held one up. As usual I didn't know the word. I'd been working with her for over two months and had made zip for progress. The same words, week after week, on flash cards and placed in stories either I dictated or she wrote, and still I never recognized them—or I recognized them but just couldn't crack them. I didn't think I'd learned anything in all our weeks working together. I guessed it was an old dog/new tricks situation.

Surely I could talk into a tape machine, I thought later that night as I drove home from PayLess with my new recorder. Talking was something I excelled at. Hustler equals talker. Lori Taylor equals mouth. Which was what Deirdre Felix was probably thinking when she gave me the assignment.

Me and my "marvelous details."

I set the tape recorder up on my hamper in the bathroom, ran a tub, then got in the steaming water. I pushed the "record" button. The tape machine started whirring and I held the microphone to my mouth but no words came out. I pushed "stop," then hit "play" and listened to ten seconds of my own heavy breathing along with the tiny splashes my feet had made.

I pushed "record" again, forced some words out of my mouth, then suddenly they flowed: "Mickey has totally checked out. He's like gone-zo. He always comes to work in a daze. Sometimes it's a giddy daze and sometimes he's all profound, like being in love is deeper for him. It's definitely not a joking matter. Before he'd slept with her he was calling me every night, telling me every single word Sheila uttered to him. But now when I ask him for deets, he acts as if sex is this sacred thing, like I offend him even asking. He barely seems to want to talk anymore and he definitely won't talk dirty." I felt tears coming on and was about to push the "stop" button again, but didn't. The recorder made me feel as if I had an audience, like someone was listening to my words, in a different way than talking to a friend. On tape, the words—my words—were permanent, fixed. I sniffed in my tears, right on tape, and went on.

"I'm doing this whole reading thing because of Mickey and he isn't even interested. I've tried telling him about Deirdre Felix a couple of times. It's sort of complicated explaining about her. She's so distant and strict, and yet she told me today that she'd asked a librarian—I wonder if it was Pam—for some books by lesbian authors because maybe they would interest me more than other books. That's pretty cool. I mean, she's this straight lady who's more than twice my age and goes to the ballet but I guess she's got more inside her than I thought. Funny, because I expected her to think of me real narrowly but actually I was the one who was thinking of her real narrowly. Anyway, Mickey listens when I try and tell him this stuff and he even comments but I can tell he couldn't care less. Even when I tried to tell him about Dr. Julie Higginboth and the sex workshop, stories he would have lapped up before, he acted all superior, like anything I'm going through is artificial compared to his life." I pushed "stop" and took a deep breath. Then I pushed "record" and said, "I miss him. I really miss Mickey."

Whitney Yarbrough called again, this time to ask if I wanted to go to the next BONG meeting. "I'd love to," I told her, "but I can't that night."

She was silent. I knew she was weighing that "I'd love to" just as I had weighed it when Pam used it on me. Was I being sincere? I wondered myself. Why didn't I just tell her not to call me again?

"Do you want me to call and tell you when the next BONG meeting is?"

I hate it when women do that, call you on your evasiveness. "Sure," I said. "Yeah. Definitely. Let's keep in touch."

I hung up and felt like a crumb. I had the guts of a flea.

When she called again a week later, this time to invite me to the Bank of the West Classic tennis tournament, I was tempted. It was Martina's last Bay Area tournament. But I told her I was going out of town. A stupid excuse because I really wanted to go and now I couldn't for fear I'd run into Whitney and she'd know I had lied to her.

"Why do you care what she thinks if you don't even like her?" Mickey asked, impatient as usual with what he perceived as my petty concerns.

It was a cold December evening and we were leaving work.

"I do like her," I told Mickey, who stopped to preen in the shop window. "She's very persistent. I like that in a woman. Shows character."

I laughed, Mickey didn't.

"Then you're playing games with her," he said, now searching up and down the street with his eyes. I realized he was waiting for *her*.

"So now you're the expert on sincerity, is that it? Do you know you've gotten very judgmental lately?"

"Get real, Lori. Yeah maybe I do like sincerity better than skimming the surface of everything. If you like the woman, go out with her. If you don't, then don't. Don't string her along."

That hurt. Mickey didn't understand and I didn't know how to begin explaining how tangled my life had become because the snarl was completely an interior thing. It was much more complicated than whether or not I liked Whitney, much more complicated than game-playing. Something inside me was getting destroyed. It was like a big wrecking ball swung back and forth in there knocking down one structure after another until I wasn't sure who I was anymore. The protective parts of me were toppling and nothing was replacing them. One old idea persisted, an idea that I guess had been there all along but I'd hidden with all my excuses: I was nobody if I couldn't read. And I definitely couldn't read. So I guess that made me nobody, nothing. I'd spent my life avoiding exposure, making sure no one saw that hole in me. As I returned week after week to my hour with Deirdre Felix, that hole opened up, grew huge. I realized it was the same opening as that craving feeling I'd had that day on the beach, that ache of desire, only now it was a crater, widening by the week. How could I go out with Whitney Yarbrough?

Enrique came out of the shop and as he locked up, asked how far behind we were in repairs.

"It's not nearly as bad as it looks," I assured him. "There are a lot of jobs up on the board but they're small ones, all of them."

Enrique hooked the keys back onto his belt loop and looked us over like we were two bad kids. The fact was, we'd never been so far behind. And December was one of our slowest months. When Mickey wasn't on the phone with Sheila, he was daydreaming about her. I spent hours working on special projects, like taking apart, oiling and reassembling shop tools and machines rather than getting orders done. I stared at Enrique's feet, which looked like two big loaves of bread, and had one of those moments of feeling totally inadequate, like I was a puff of hot air next to his mass. I always had this urge to feel his parts, like one of his bulky thighs or arms, like maybe if I took hold of him I would glean important information about making ideas materialize.

I rarely looked Enrique in the eye, partly because his eyes were so far up there and partly because I got hung up on his impressive body, but now I swept my gaze upward until I found those two green windows. Green like Deirdre Felix's plants which knew how to make their own food. Green like money.

As if cued to my thoughts, Enrique pulled out his wallet and unfolded two fresh checks. He handed one to each of us. "Christmas bonus. And I want the board cleared by Friday."

Enrique strode away, his keys jangling off his belt loop.

Mickey's face lit up and I raised a hand for a high five, whooping, "Let's celebrate!"

Then I saw the girl coming up the sidewalk and realized his face was for her, not for the check. She wore army boots and a short tiny-flower print dress which, with the flurry of freckles on her face, made her look, at this distance, entirely polka-dotted. She carried a knapsack packed with lots of square bookish shapes over one shoulder. Her big breasts bounced as she walked. She needed a better bra.

Oh Mickey. I looked at my friend who, if he weren't working so hard at being butch these days, would have done the Clairol thing and gone leaping toward Sheila. My heart went out to him and out to me at the same time. We'd thrust each other into these new lives. Had we made huge mistakes?

"Okay, Mick," I said, trying to get his attention for one last second. "I'm going. But you know, I guess you're right. I should be more direct with Whitney."

"See you tomorrow," Mickey said, swaggering off to meet his girlfriend. He must have felt me watching his back because he stopped and turned. "You okay?" he asked and when I shook my head no, he returned and gave me a hug. I held him tight until he disengaged and said, "It's time for one of our phô dinners soon. We'll celebrate with our checks."

"I'd like that," I said, wondering how he could believe that eating bowls of Vietnamese noodle soup together would mend all that had begun to go wrong, even if it was a tradition of ours. "When?"

"Soon," he called over his shoulder. A moment later he took his big teenage girlfriend into his arms.

I watched the lovers float down the street until they became as small as birds.

That night I decided to give Edith a try. I found her new number and called.

"Remember me?" I asked, then listened to a string of scrambled excuses for why she'd been out of touch for so long though we both knew it was because of her recent merger. To lure her interest, knowing she absorbed anything about love, I told her I was dating a librarian. She said she'd like to see me and we made a date for her next available evening which was in three weeks.

Then I went to try, for the last time, to make my dating-a-librarian story true. If Pam said no again, I'd quit.

It was a Monday night so I didn't have to risk Lillian sabotaging me again. Charles, that guy who read with his finger, was there, but I knew he wouldn't speak to me. I didn't see her right away but found her alone in the stacks. She wore a fluffy blue sweater and. . . .

My god. Why hadn't I noticed that bulge at her belly before tonight?

"Hey," she said. "How's it going? The shelver is out sick so I'm stuck putting the books away."

"You're pregnant," I accused.

She smiled warmly, even matronly, already full of secret knowledge. "Yes," she gushed.

"You're straight?"

"Of course not."

"You have a partner?" I pressed with the question I should have asked a couple of months ago.

"Yes," she said, not quite so enthusiastically. The sneaky look around the corners of her eyes told me she knew she'd been leading me on.

"And I bet you've even had a commitment ceremony." Just a hunch.

She beamed.

For the first time I noticed that she had oversized teeth, yellowish too. Her once short-short hair wasn't so short anymore. It was growing out thin and sparse. Was it my imagination or do lesbians who have babies grow out their hair and begin to dress straighter? Her eagerness, so endearing in past weeks, seemed goofy in the harsh light of my anger.

"Have fun in the nursery," I said, turning away.

"Wait a minute! Why the sarcasm?"

"*Pfft*," I said, imitating Deirdre Felix. I walked over to the sports section—she did not follow me—and chose a book with a bicycle on the cover. I flipped through the pages and found drawings of different bicycle parts, stuff I knew inside and out, which kindled my confidence. I headed for the door with my book.

I jumped about ten feet when the alarm sounded. I dropped the book, panicked, picked it up again. I turned in a full circle like I was surrounded. I felt the same way I did that time in ninth grade when I got busted in the school bathroom for smoking dope. Pam's voice sounded like it was coming down a long tunnel when she said, "It's your book setting off the alarm. You forgot to check it out."

I don't know why I bolted but I did. Clenching my bicycle repair book, I plowed through the door and covered a full three blocks before realizing that my car was parked in the library lot. I decided to leave it there and get it later that night, after I could be sure Pam had left. I continued walking up University Avenue and when I came to my own street, passed it and kept on walking until I reached Shattuck Avenue. There I caught a bus heading south towards Oakland. Deirdre Felix, who I noticed took buses to and from all our meetings now, must have to transfer at least two times to get home from the library. Why didn't she just take cabs? Did buses even run up into the hills? I walked to the front of the bus and asked the driver, "Hey, how do you get up to Skyline Boulevard on the bus?"

"This bus goes to downtown Oakland."

"I know that. But say I wanted to get up in the hills. How would I do that?"

He nodded to a sheath of papers in a leather pouch next to the fare dispenser. "Schedules there."

"Thanks." I leafed through the schedules, pretended I'd found the one I needed and walked to the back of the bus again. I laid on my back in the ragged seat and felt as empty as this old bus rattling up Shattuck Avenue. I watched the street lights and billboards blink by and to keep my mind off pregnant and married

Pam, tried to concentrate on how Deirdre Felix could get home by bus from the library. Before I knew it we were at the bus terminal in Oakland where the bus driver told me I had to get off, it was the end of his run.

I didn't have enough money for a cab, not even for another bus fare and I didn't think to ask the driver for a transfer until it was too late. I sat in the bus station with a lot of homeless people and called Mickey every half hour, quickly using up the seventy-five cents in my pocket. I left him three messages to come get me but I didn't expect to see him. I sat upright on a bench and wondered what Deirdre Felix would think of her student passing a night in the Oakland bus station for no reason at all. At this very moment she was probably directly east of me and fifteen hundred feet above me, up there in her home on the crest of the Oakland hills, sipping wine and watching TV. No, she'd be reading a book or discussing art and politics with Arnie.

At one in the morning Mickey burst through the bus terminal doorway looking real angry. I'd never seen his face twisted in that particular way. I felt like his daughter whom he'd caught hooking. He actually said, "Get in the car."

We rode to my house in silence because I didn't know what to say and sensed, strongly, that he didn't want to hear it anyway. Before I got out of the car I reached over to hug him. He put one arm around me, loosely. "What's going on, Lori?" he finally asked sounding more annoyed than concerned. "You're acting so weird."

I couldn't explain myself but I did know he was acting as weirdly as me. Before, he might have been mad but he would have laughed, he would have demanded to know how I got stuck in downtown Oakland, he would have known I would have a good answer. Of course tonight I didn't have a good answer. "Good night," was all I said and, "Thank you."

10

MARILYN, THE DIRECTOR of the Literacy Project, said that tutors and learners should meet in neutral places like the library, but Deirdre Felix suggested we meet at her house if I didn't mind.

I didn't mind. In fact, I was relieved. The timing could not have been better. I didn't want to see Pam ever again, the sneaky little tease. All those wasted months. I wish women would just say, "You fuckhead, why do you think I would ever go out with you?" instead of, "That sounds like so much fun, but this is such a busy time for me." I guess I could take a hint but I chose to believe she meant she would like to have all that fun as soon as she was not so busy.

Even so, the night I was supposed to go to Deirdre Felix's house, I missed Pam acutely. I didn't want to see her but I did want my fantasies of her. I guess I had ridden my lust like a train right up to each reading session at the library. Now I had to go cold. It would be me and Deirdre Felix, me and the reading.

I was late because I had trouble finding her Oakland hills

house through the sheets of rain. Up there it's like wilderness, black forests and no street lights, a little too natural for me, at least at night.

I arrived at six-forty-five, parked in the street, then navigated a winding flagstone walkway through a forest-sized garden to her porch. Before ringing the bell I turned and looked at the huge plants towering over the flagstone walk, their branches bending and dripping rainwater. Why didn't she live somewhere regular, like in a nice apartment building or a house with a simple lawn? Big thunder rolled across the sky as I rang the doorbell. I shuddered and expected Lurch to open the door.

Deirdre Felix wore a dark green fleece pullover, tan khakis and penny loafers. Her casualness threw me—where were the blazer and flannel slacks? The hallway smelled like fresh cut timber and glowed with a dark woody warmth. As she hustled me along to her study, I peered into all the rooms. Oriental rugs covered the floors and real paintings hung on the walls. There were lots of art objects sitting on fancy little tables. A huge Christmas tree partially decorated with old-fashioned, probably antique, ornaments stood in the living room. More ornament boxes were strewn around the tree. I wondered if Arnie had been helping her decorate the tree or if the architect son would be home for Christmas. Someone was blasting classical music in a room upstairs.

"Where'd you get all this art?" I asked.

"Mostly from our travels."

"Where have you traveled to?"

Deirdre Felix didn't like answering questions, at least not mine. Sometimes I would have liked just a tiny cushion of friendly conversation between me and The Lesson. But no. She was an incredibly focused woman and with me her focus was tutoring.

As we reached a large redwood door, which was closed, she said, "I appreciate your willingness to meet here. I'm temporarily out of a car."

"I know," I said and felt embarrassed for not having thought of making it easier on her myself. "How did you get to the library by bus, anyway?"

"*Pfft*," she said.

"What happened to your car?" I tried.

Some emotion—anger? disgust? fear?—seized her face for a second. "Totaled," she said.

"Are you okay? Were you driving?"

"I'm fine," she said as she opened the big door and led me into a hostile-looking room she called her study. The chairs were too big and too padded. The fire in the fireplace looked almost out of control, noisily consuming half a tree trunk. I glanced around looking for a fire extinguisher and did not see one. All four walls of this room were floor-to-ceiling bookshelves packed with books. They gave me vertigo. I stood in the doorway, feeling attached to the classical music drifting through the house to my ears, as if it were an incoming wave I could catch on its way back out again.

"Would you shut the door please?" Deirdre Felix asked as she sat at a mean-looking table, heavy and darkly-stained. She seemed too small for this study, like a mouse making a home in a bear's den. Yet I felt certain it wasn't Arnie's study. The way the door had been definitively closed, the way she occupied this fierce room, pulling herself up to the table, her back trustfully turned to the blaze in the fireplace, I knew she felt more at home here than in any other room in the house. Here in this tomb of books, furnished with oversized chairs, a desk and this brutish table, she took comfort of some sort. I saw it in her posture, the relaxation of her jaw, a looseness in her whole body I hadn't seen before. It made me want to sit close to her.

I shut the door, cutting off the current of music.

"The tea," she said and got up again. Deirdre Felix poured scalding water from a hotpot into a mug and handed it to me. "It's licorice," she said.

"The tea?"

"Yes. You sit there." She pointed at the end of the table. "How's the journal going?"

"Fine," I answered honestly. I had been talking into the

recorder for at least five minutes and often more every evening. I actually liked it, creating something with words, and I was pleased to report a success. I had even made a special tape for her, one that described "marvelous details" I had noticed in the shop at work. I couldn't let her listen to my real tapes because I talked about her too much. I pulled her special tape out of my pocket.

"Oh I don't want to hear it." *Pfft* went her lips and she brushed aside the air in front of her face. The insignificance of my tape I guess. Anyone could talk. "The tape is just for you," she said and handed me the same story I had tried unsuccessfully to read last week. She had written down the hard words and we had spent most of the hour working on them. The idea was that I would be able to breeze through the story this week.

I began reading. To my amazement I got through the first couple of sentences but then got stuck on the word *endurance* for the bizillionth time. Deirdre Felix sighed. "Never mind," she said, taking the story out of my hands. She dropped it on the table, got up, walked over to one of the bookshelves, and with her hands on her hips looked over the books.

I sat very still. She didn't want to hear my tape. I couldn't read the story. What now?

The wind blew rain against the window pane, making it sound as if someone outside was tapping to be let in. A bolt of lightning lit the study. Deirdre Felix, scowling at her bookcases, looked demonic in the electric light. There was something incongruous about the small, older woman and this shadowy cell built of books. It was possible that she was some kind of serial killer who lured adult learners to her study. When her frustration at their incompetence reached a certain pitch . . .

I jumped when Deirdre Felix said, "Here. This one." She pulled a book from the bookshelf and settled into one of the big padded chairs. She waved to the other one. "You'd be more comfortable over there."

I got up from the table and lowered myself into the chair.

"Just listen," she ordered. She expected me to sit, drink this weird tea and listen to her read.

I didn't listen very well. The words all blurred together. I watched her face and wondered where Arnie was. What else she did in this study. Who had been the driver of the Beamer that had infuriated her. Who had totaled her Saab. Why, since I clearly annoyed her, she bothered. Why, since I obviously was making no progress, I bothered.

Yet here I was in this strange study, listening to this distracted, seemingly sorrowful woman.

Sometimes the fire flared up and threw bursts of light into the study. As she read, I smiled at my picture of her as demonic. Hardly. She leaned against the arm of her chair, toward the fire, and read quietly, her gray eyes flinty in the firelight, her brow jumping on certain words, not a smile but a warmth on her thin lips, a warmth like memory. She had a small nose, the kind that would have been called pert in high school, and full cheeks that looked like little pillows. I could tell she liked the story she was reading. Another gust of wind shook the windows and she smiled as she read the words, " . . . the branch of a fir tree that touched my lattice, as the blast wailed by, and rattled its dry cones against the panes . . . "

I looked nervously at the window, listened to the tapping, wondered if it was caused by dry cones, then tried to listen to what she read, but the words were old-fashioned and I was too full of the fire's heat, the licorice flavor coating my tongue, the *sounds* of the words rather than the meanings of them. She had an easy voice and it lulled me into my own thoughts.

When she finished reading I thought she would ask me questions to test my comprehension, and I was as bad at that as I was at decoding words, but I was wrong. When our hour was up, she shut the book and looked at me. She could see I had been spacing out. "See you next week?" she asked.

I stood. I ought to tell her this wasn't working. It was a waste of her time. She had been happy just now reading in this room, but I felt tied and gagged with words, bound in by these four walls of books, my inability to concentrate on her reading. I followed her back down the long hallway and left without speaking.

Three days later, on Saturday morning, Deirdre Felix called me. The sun had come out and although it was chilly, I lay in bed on my stomach with the cottage door open. A pungent wet earth smell filled my room and a cold sunshine poured in the door. In front of me on the bed, in a pie tin, were all the itsy bitsy parts of my father's watch which I'd taken apart for fun, just to see if I could put it back together again. Unless I got one of those magnifying glasses you strap to your eye and fingers the size of toothpicks, I did not think I was going to succeed.

I clenched the phone between my shoulder and jaw and continued tinkering with the watch.

"I have to go out of town for a few weeks," she said. "I'm not exactly sure for how long but I expect to be home by mid-January. We should miss only three meetings."

"No problem," I said, amazed by my immediate disappointment. Shouldn't I be relieved? "Where are you going?"

"My sister's in New York. I'll call you when I get back."

"Okey-dokey," I said, forcing cheerfulness and hung up. I knew she wouldn't call when she came back. I guess everyone in the world was a coward at heart. Pam couldn't tell me the truth about her partner and baby, I couldn't tell Whitney Yarbrough that I didn't want to date her and even Deirdre Felix, from whom I had expected exacting honesty if nothing else, was too chicken to tell me she didn't want to tutor me anymore.

That was okay. That was fine. Actually that was *good,* it was like release from brain prison. I celebrated by carrying the stack of flash cards out to the garbage can and dumping them. Then I rode my bike to Cactus Taqueria and devoured a super vegetarian food log. After that I rode to the only real watch shop left in the Bay Area, now that nearly every watch is digital, and bought one of those magnifying glasses and a tiny pair of tweezers. The guy thought I was crazy. "It'd be cheaper just to have me fix your watch," he said, then way overcharged me for the tools. It was worth it though. I spent all afternoon putting those miniature springs, wheels and arms back together and you know, by six o'clock I had that thing ticking.

The next Wednesday evening I was restless. Once rats get used to a route, they will run along it no matter what obstacles are put in their way. All animals do that. Like the caribou in Alaska who jump right over the pipeline everyone worried about so much. I guess I had gotten that way about Wednesdays and tutoring. In spite of the discomfort and feelings of restriction, I had grown accustomed to spending that time with Deirdre Felix. I liked watching the way she warmed up to books and was intrigued by how she had slipped into another world in that dark, heavy study. I didn't much like reading books but I had begun to like reading Deirdre Felix. Trying to anyway.

As the evening wore on I could not stop thinking about her, wondering if she really did go to New York. If she had, and if she did call me again in three weeks, I would feel awful about trashing the flash cards. I even sort of missed them, the feel of those big square cards in my hands—not the brain crunching feeling of trying to read them but the actual bulk of the stack in my hands, the way one card slid over the next, the way I set aside the words I finally had learned, knew cold, and how they became a tiny stack of their own, my little victory pile.

I channel-surfed for an hour, made myself gourmet scrambled eggs, meaning I added garlic powder and onion flakes, and listened a number of times to Mickey's answering machine message. He never answered his phone anymore. At work last week I had explained about Pam, the library book I accidentally stole and my bus ride. He had laughed at the right places, but then remarked that none of that explained why I was at the Oakland bus station in the middle of the night, and changed the subject.

By ten o'clock I had to do something to ease my restlessness, so I took my mountain bike down from its hook and rode across town. Moving, moving fast in the night, felt good. Though it wasn't raining, the air was wet and cold. I had told Whitney that I often rode at night but I lied. I never ride at night. It's dangerous and stupid. I didn't have lights or even reflectors on my bike. I knew the cars couldn't see me until they were upon me and tonight I enjoyed that, feeling like a ghost, invisible. I had only one near-hit and that was long after I had left town and started up Tunnel Road into the hills. I heard the screeching tires a few turns down the hill and knew it was probably some drunk kids and that I should get off my bike and wait beside the road until they passed. I didn't do that. I kept riding until I heard them squeal around the turn directly behind me. The steel of the car door brushed my leg, just barely, like a metal kiss, as it passed. I don't think the driver even knew I was there.

At the top, where Grizzly Peak Road comes in, I continued south, riding along the crest of the hills on Skyline Boulevard. The moon was three-quarters full, throwing off plenty of light where the trees didn't crowd the road.

When I got there, I stopped at the beginning of the flagstone walkway and stood straddling my bike trying to see through the vegetation to the house. There were definitely lights on. As I watched, two blinked off. That tan Beamer was in the driveway.

I stashed my bike under a bush with red berries, then walked right up the flagstones. What did I think I was going to do, ring the bell? When I got to the porch, I stepped into the garden and squeezed between two trees to the side of the house. The soil beneath my feet was soft and wet and I realized I had left the garden and entered the woods. I was perched on the side of a damp bank and could hear, not more than ten feet below me, the trickling of a creek. Up ahead, a golden square of light cast a warm glow onto the evergreens. I inched my way along the bank toward that window and when I got there, peered into a kitchen. A young blond woman—a young and stunning blond woman—wearing a midnight blue evening dress was smearing a brown paste on little rounds of bread. She arranged them on a small, lacy plate, then picked up an open bottle of red wine and left the kitchen. Deirdre Felix hadn't mentioned a daughter. Maybe the son's wife? Deirdre Felix would not go to New York for Christmas if her son and daughter-in-law were visiting.

I sunk down below the window and leaned against the house, suddenly breathless. I had one of those mirror moments in which you see yourself doing something unthinkable. And yet you must continue doing it. Mickey—my earnest and honorable friend Mickey—would truly disown me if he knew I was spying on people.

Yet I needed to know if Deirdre Felix was home or not, I needed to know if she had lied to me, so I crawled to the back of the house where I hoped to get another view inside. Just as I rounded the corner, keeping low by moving like a crab on all fours, a furry bulk brushed along my shoulder and arm. I screamed and leapt away from the house.

A bank of floodlights flashed on, gestapo style. I froze for an instant, blinking into the intense light, then dove into the woods behind the house. I tripped on a log and fell into a bed of wet leaves and pine needles where I laid on my belly as still as I could.

A door must have opened because faint classical music spilled into the night. Then I heard a man's deep voice, "Hello? Who is it? Hello? Hello?"

As I laid in the outer perimeter of the pool of light, I felt the wet soil seeping into my wool cycling jersey and tights. I wasn't too pleased with the idea of anyone in the Felix family finding me pressed against the forest floor in their backyard, but the idea of that furry animal—an opossum? a raccoon?—returning made me sick. I shifted the weight of one thigh and something hard and snake-like whipped against my knee. A long scaly opossum tail. I stifled a gag. The hard thing stayed on the back of my knee until I realized that no forest creature would willingly snuggle up to a human. I reached back and knocked the stick off my leg.

A minute later the lights switched off again. I thought it best to wait a good long time before moving but when I heard rustling a couple of feet away, I got up fast. I stayed as close to the house as I could so as not to trigger the floodlight sensors again and worked my way to the front garden where I hoped to crawl through the thick plants to my bike. As I squeezed between the two trees, the lights jumped on again, so I lunged for the walkway where I would be visible but could move fast, and sprinted to the street.

I dragged my bike out from under the red-berried bush, climbed on and pedaled hard. If that man with the deep voice or that blond babe called the police, I could be dead. Don't police love shooting at moving targets? I descended Tunnel Road like a maniac, swinging wide on the turns to keep myself from crashing, my inside pedal sparking as it scraped the pavement, and hoped for no oncoming traffic. My heart pumped so much adrenaline through my system I could have ridden the Tour de France that night.

By the time I got home, my feet felt like blocks of ice and my chest heaved with cold exertion. I locked myself in my cottage and hung up my bike. I ran steaming hot water into the clawfoot tub, climbed in and cried. I don't know why I cried, but I cried and cried and cried.

11

"GOOD MORNING," I TOLD my tape recorder, "this is a report from Central Control. We have now officially crossed over into looney land. I've become a prowler. One thing for which we can be grateful: Mickey used to accuse me of putting everything in sexual terms. Well, I've moved on to other perversions like lurking in urban bus stations and spying on people in their homes at night.

"What else do I have to report? Besides practicing for my next career as a burglar, not much. I'm gonna see Edith tonight. Our big date. Whoopdeedoo. It'll be an hour and a half of lovesick—emphasis on sick—stories, then she'll have to run. They've been together for six months now. You'd think the gaga stage would be over. I'll put money on Edith having gained about ten pounds—she always does when she gets into a new relationship—and her swearing that this one is 'totally different.' I'll hear how she's finally broken old patterns, how good this new one—what's her name?—is for her, blah, blah, blah.

"Oh cut the shit, Lori. It'll be good to see Edith. I'm looking forward to it."

The phone rang. I stopped recording and listened to my phone machine take the call. I heard Edith explain that she and her girlfriend were coming down with colds. She knew I would understand and what if we rescheduled for Wednesday night, February twentieth? She was dying to catch up with me. Give her a call.

"Rule number one about dating," I told Mickey in the bike shop later that day. "Don't desert your friends while you're in love. The main difference between friends and lovers is that lovers leave. Friends don't, if you treat them right."

Mickey lifted a bike onto the stand as he said, "Get a life, Lori."

I threw my wrench down on the cement floor. "Damn you, Mickey. Just because you're fucking that fat teenager doesn't mean you're suddenly an authority on life. And just because I'm not doing anything but going to work and talking to myself on a tape recorder doesn't mean things aren't happening to me." I startled myself by collapsing onto the floor next to my wrench and breaking into sobs.

"Lori! God I'm sorry."

I could not stop crying once I had started. Mickey patted my shoulder. He had never seen me cry.

"You're the one who said sex wasn't everything," I blubbered. "You're so pussy-whipped you don't even think about your bike shop anymore."

Mickey sat on the floor next to me and I put my face on his wool plaid shoulder. He put both arms around me. He didn't say anything more and let me cry until Enrique came into the repair room.

"Lori, Mickey, I need some help on—" I heard Enrique's voice above my sobs. I looked up and saw his big presence in the doorway. My glasses were in my lap so he was all blurry but I could tell

92

he was shocked to see me and Mickey embracing on the cement floor.

"Could we have a minute?" Mickey said and Enrique disappeared. A moment later he returned and dropped a box of Kleenex on the floor in front of me, then left again.

"I'm sorry, Mick. I don't know what's wrong with me." Up close Mickey was beautiful with eyes as sweet and seductive as chocolate, with that nutty asymmetrical mouth. I leaned into him.

"Did something happen with your librarian friend? What was her name? Paula?"

"Pam. No. I told you. Nothing happened with her at all."

"Oh, I see."

"No, you don't see!" I started boohoohooing all over again, holding Mickey's thin muscular arms, wondering how I could make him understand. Yes, it hurt that Pam had rejected me. But it hurt more that Deirdre Felix had. I hated admitting that even to myself.

"We could go out to dinner tonight," he said. "I'll buy. We'll do our phô dinner."

It was such a simple offer, at once what I needed and missing the point entirely. Everything missed the point these days. The point was too big.

"Promise you won't order tripe or fish eyeball phô," I said. "You always make me lose my appetite."

"I promise."

"Okay," I muttered, then added pitifully, "but if you have plans with Sheila, we can do it tomorrow night or some other time."

"Uh, no," he said, but not before I noticed the micro-hesitation in his voice. "We'll do it tonight."

A few minutes later he was on the telephone in the back corner murmuring his excuses to Sheila.

The Vietnamese noodle soup dinner with Mickey restored my humor. I gave him a hard time about growing out his hair. It was now long enough—just—to wear in a short ponytail held back with a leather thong. He had to keep sweeping his bangs, which would not yet fit into the leather thong, out of his eyes. I hoped very much that Sheila loved him as much as he loved her.

By the end of dinner Mickey had talked me into asking Whitney Yarbrough out. "What could it hurt?" he wanted to know. "You like her, right?"

"Right," I answered.

As I drove home I decided on rule number two about dating: If your friends desert you while they're in love, start dating someone yourself.

I called her later that night and she answered before the end of the first ring. I suggested dinner Friday night. She was silent for a moment, which didn't surprise me. She had to be wondering why I'd changed my mind about going out with her. She rose to the occasion though, saying, "I'll cook you dinner."

"I'm taking you out to dinner." This date was on my terms and I was paying. Pacing was everything and I wanted to be the one running the show.

I took Whitney to a classy and expensive Italian restaurant in the Oakland hills not too far from where Deirdre Felix lived. I did feel a little sleazy about my motives. Had I asked Whitney out because I knew she would say yes? Because Pam had rejected me and I needed a hit of acceptance? Maybe. But not entirely. Whitney was a daunting woman, very accomplished and on the verge of more accomplishment. It was easier now that Deirdre Felix and my weekly dumbo sessions with flash cards were gone to feel like her equal. And to reclaim my Don Juanita persona.

Whitney looked nice that night. She wore a raw silk tawny jumpsuit, great with her blond hair, a black belt and black heels. Heels! I wouldn't have expected as much from tame Whitney Yarbrough and I was pleased. What other surprises might she reveal? In a way it was more fun dating a woman I didn't have a heavy crush on. I could orchestrate what happened rather than be washed along by the drama of my feeling.

I got through the menu without a hitch. "Which salad do you recommend?" "What's the fish tonight?" "Great, I'll take that." Casual and butch, that's how I came off. Whitney studied her menu for a long time and ordered by the exact names of the dishes. I told her to choose the wine she wanted and she picked something red.

She told me a lot about her greeting cards, her graphic design business and her father. Her mother died of cancer a year ago at which time her last girlfriend dumped her and she hadn't dated since. My rescue fantasies flared and I warned myself to chill, reminded myself that Whitney was far from helpless. She asked about my family and I told the truth about everything. My mom lived in Barstow in the Mohave Desert with her third husband. My father left when I was fourteen and he called me every six months to a year. I told her that I really loved my dad and that I learned everything important I know from him. "This is his watch." I held up my wrist to show her the silver man's watch.

"But you don't ever see him?"

"We talk."

"Once a year?"

"Sometimes more often."

I knew what she was driving at. I was not supposed to adore the man who had left me and my mother, the father whom I rarely, actually never, saw. Like Mom, Whitney probably thought it was one-sided, my feelings for my father. It wasn't. I knew he loved me. I didn't really know the details of why he left and I had never asked my mother, partly because I knew I would get a heavily-biased answer, but I am my father's daughter and know what it's like to not be able to carry through with something. Mom doesn't. Her middle name is Purpose. She leaps from one goal to the next like stepping stones. One year it's rug-making, another it's selling Nu Skin. I love my mother too but her accomplishments pile up around her like a barricade. She's harder to know than my father even though I talk to her every couple of weeks.

We each ordered an espresso—Whitney got decaf—and we shared a dessert of cannelloni stuffed with fancy sweet cheeses, drizzled with a bitter-sweet chocolate sauce and sprinkled with fresh raspberries.

"How's the bike shop coming along?" she asked.

"Good," I said and stuffed more chocolaty cheese into my mouth hoping that would stifle her next question.

"Tell me where you are with it."

It had been a couple of months since that BONG meeting. A lot should have happened. It hadn't. I let myself get distracted by the quarter-inch of freckled cleavage showing just above the top button of her fawn-colored jumpsuit.

"Have you found a space yet?" Whitney asked.

After a quick mental scramble I realized I could just tell the truth. "My business partner—Mickey—fell in love. It's kind of stalled everything."

"What a drag!" she said too heartfully, making me wonder why she cared so much about my nonexistent bike shop.

To change the subject I suggested an after dinner drive. I even opened the car door for her which I could tell by the way she said "Oh please!" and grabbed the door handle to pull it shut herself was a little too corny, or maybe too butchy, for her.

I drove up Tunnel Road and then out Skyline. "Kinda scary out here, isn't it?" I said.

"It's nice. I like it."

When we got to Deirdre Felix's house I pulled over. I wondered what Whitney would say or think if I told her that this was my tutor's house, that I was—or had been—learning to read, just now at age twenty-eight. I said, "It'd be nice to have a house like that, wouldn't it?"

"So much greenery!"

"I'll say." I tried to see through the greenery to the house. Lights were on again.

For a moment I felt as if my car were a cage, maybe it was my whole life, a cage that had always been there but I hadn't been able to see until I met Deirdre Felix. Now I felt like all I could do was grip the bars and shake, and I didn't want to be doing that, gripping and shaking. I wanted my old life back. I wanted the gauzy, padded perimeter—not attention to detail. I rolled down a window, took a big gulp of the cold winter air, said, "Yeah, a whole lot of greenery."

I released the parking brake, turned the car around and drove back down Tunnel Road. I had thought of taking Whitney to one of the regional park turn-outs but there would be too many teenagers making out in cars. Kind of tacky for a first date.

"Want to come in?" Whitney asked when we got to her house. "I rented a couple of videos."

"Thanks," I said, unnerved by her forwardness and advance planning, "but I got a lot of stuff to do tomorrow."

I saw that lurch backwards in her eyes. Whitney wasn't a game-player. Her face showed everything. I wanted to touch her cheek, bring her eyes forward again, tell her she did not have to be frightened of me. I heard myself adding, "What about a bike ride on Sunday? You and your Bianchi."

"Okay," she said, sounding unsure. My voice had a swagger to it that very sincere women like Whitney didn't always trust.

"Good. Is the morning okay? Meet me at the reservoir at the top of Spruce—you know the beginning of Wildcat Canyon? Say nine o'clock. We'll ride out the paved trail from Inspiration Point."

I couldn't help noticing the little twitch in her slightly pouty lower lip. I touched her chin, just barely, as I said good night.

Whitney beat me to the reservoir even though, for once, I was early. She wore sleek black biker shorts and a red fleece jacket. I propped my bike against the stop sign and helped her unload her Bianchi. I had brought my tools, guessing that her bike would need a bit of work, and I was right, it did. I cleaned and oiled the chain, put air in the tires, tightened the brakes and made a small adjustment to the derailleur—this last more to show off than because it needed it. Handling tools gave me a dead center calm, a feeling of deep satisfaction. Once I got a taste of that feeling, I hated leaving it. I got kind of obsessive. I wanted to go home with Whitney and fix everything in her apartment.

Instead we strapped on helmets and I snapped my feet into Look pedals. I set a brisk pace to impress her.

"Slow down," she called out.

"You go ahead," I said. "I'll go your pace." She had this cute determined set to her jaw as she rode past me.

Mickey was smart in counseling me to ask Whitney out. It felt right, more than right, it felt good. So had throwing out the flash cards. And the two *were* related. Whitney Yarbrough made me feel butch, meaning smart and tough and in control. Deirdre Felix, at least what I did with her, made me feel scared and empty and out of control. I had thrown away the flash cards and didn't want to think about her anymore. Without Deirdre Felix in my face week after week I could believe I had more in common with Whitney Yarbrough than I had with Charles and Lillian.

When Whitney and I got to Inspiration Point we rode out the paved path, taking in the spectacular views of the bay and all the bridges, stark against the winter blue sky. We rode for several miles out to where the pavement ends. Since we had brought road rather than mountain bikes we couldn't ride any further.

"Come on," I told her. "Follow me." I pushed my bike up a dirt path to the top of a grassy knoll, then across the knoll to a spot where we could look out over Richmond, the bay, all of Marin and places north.

I put down my bike and nestled into the pale grasses.

"Do you race?" she asked, sitting beside me.

"Nah."

She touched the skin just above my knee. "Big biking muscles."

I stared out at Mount Tamalpais, pretending to be looking at something specific, working up my nerve. Then I turned, too quickly, and kissed her bottom lip. I surprised her and she jerked back a little. I laid back in the grass, willed my trembling to stop and looked up at the sky. Two hawks circled in the pale blue soup.

My eyes were closed when I felt her hand touch my sternum, then drift down to my belly where the fingers hesitated, then lifted the bottom of my jersey and touched my skin. I opened my eyes. She laid down beside me, propped up on one elbow, hovering. I was used to being in charge romantically and I wasn't sure I liked her position above me. She leaned closer and kissed my mouth.

It was a sweet kiss.

When she pulled away I breathed in the straw grass around our heads and felt something in my chest blow open like a gust of wind through my lungs. I sat up and gently nudged her onto her back. She smiled at me, shy but definitely lustful. It was the sexual version of that ambivalence I'd seen in her, the way she could be uncertain and tentative and yet determined and sure. She pushed me back on my shoulder blades and kissed me again.

No woman had ever pushed me on my back, not forcefully, not without my prior consent. I counseled myself to end this kiss but I did not. We did not stop kissing and still I was on my back. Whitney placed her knee between my legs. And I let her.

I let her a lot.

12

"Whoa," I told my tape recorder minutes before Whitney was due for dinner. Though it was still January, I had bought chicken and some veggies to barbecue on my landlady's grill. "This thing with Whitney is moving so fast. It's only been a couple of weeks but it feels like it's been a few months.

"What can I say. Mickey's doing it. Edith's doing it. Why shouldn't I? I gotta admit it feels good to be immersed in something so human. Especially after a few months of nothing but TV, work and word-busting. It seems like sex is the only thing left in life that's purely biological. And Whitney and I definitely have a nice time in bed. Surprised me. We're so different. I expected her to be a lot tamer, more reserved.

"Mmm. Then there're those big doe eyes of hers. Sweet but almost scary. Like they're very inviting but I don't know what exactly is behind them. And like one thing could be behind the right eye, another behind the left one. Door number one and door number two. I choose for the prize.

"Am I falling in love? Definitely getting drawn in. Somehow."

I heard the knock on my door, hit the "stop" button, then for fun hit "record" again. I slid the tape player under my bed, opened the door and greeted Whitney.

"Hi sweetie," she said, giving me a kiss.

"Sweetie?"

"Oh loosen up. I can call you 'sweetie' if I want."

"I guess you can," I said, "but I don't know if you can leave this here." I took her toothbrush, which she had left in my bathroom, out of my back pocket and held it in her face. Dogs pee in corners to claim territory and women leave toothbrushes.

"I forgot it," she said, snatching the toothbrush out of my hand. "An accident, okay?"

What really scared me was that I was only mildly edgy about Whitney leaving her toothbrush. During the three days I had had it, I brushed my teeth twice as often as usual and used her toothbrush every time.

"I have a surprise," she said.

"What?" The way her eyes glittered I thought she had pierced her nipple or brought champagne.

She opened the big black canvas bag she always carried and pulled out a laptop computer. "Where's an outlet?"

"What are you doing?"

"We're going to write the first draft of your business plan. It'll get you and Mickey going."

I tried to speak as Whitney bustled around my cottage looking for an outlet. "I can't believe you don't even have a table," she said. "Where do you eat? Where do you write?" She found an outlet next to the bed. "This will do. It'll be cozy. We can sit together on the bed and work."

Then she saw my face which felt like skin stretched on a rack. "Lori, it'll be fun! We can get a draft out in two hours. Just wait, you'll feel so relieved to get it done."

"No."

"Lori—"

"No."

"I just thought—"

"We're having an affair. I didn't hire you to be my personal manager."

The phone rang and to get out of the conversation I answered it.

"Lori, how are you?"

It was Deirdre Felix.

I turned my back to Whitney. "Fine."

"Well, I'm back in town. I'm sorry I was gone a week longer than planned. I'd like to schedule our next meeting."

"I'm kind of busy right now."

"Let's be quick then. What about this Wednesday? We can resume Wednesday evenings, if that works for you."

Whitney circled around so that she stood in front of me and could see my face.

"I don't know if I can right now."

"Why not?"

"It's not a good time. Can I call you back?"

Deirdre Felix hesitated, then said, "Yes of course. I'll look forward to hearing from you soon." She hit the word soon with emphasis. I hung up. A mist of sweat covered my face.

"Who was that?" Whitney asked.

I could not think of a single lie about who Deirdre Felix might be.

Whitney took a step back from me. "Look, Lori. We've only been seeing each other a couple weeks and I know we don't have any agreements, but I would like to know if you're seeing other women. I'd prefer if we were honest with each other."

"I'm not seeing anyone else," I said dully. "It was just someone from work. They want me to work extra hours. That's all."

She didn't look a hundred percent convinced but she did look mollified. I wanted to be angry. I would have been in the past. Who did Whitney think she was demanding to know who I talked to, who I saw? But I wasn't angry. I was confused. I wished

Whitney wasn't so damn honest. Her honesty came from the inside out, like that pink flush on her skin. I wished I could tell her about Deirdre Felix but I just couldn't. Not yet.

The laptop, now plugged in, sat purring on my bed. I bent down and yanked out the plug.

"Hey, that's bad for the computer."

I walked over to Whitney, kissed her collarbone and quickly unbuttoned her cotton shirt. She moaned on the third kiss. I loved that about Whitney, the way she gave herself over to pleasure instantly. And fully.

An hour later we laid on our backs, limp and naked on the bed. "I love you," Whitney said and I tensed until she added, "at least I do when we're making love." She laughed, so I rolled up against her and laughed too.

Then, out of the blue, she announced, "I've been offered a job with a big shot graphics firm."

"A job? Why would you do that? Your own graphics company is taking off."

"Oh I know. I won't take it." Her voice escaped her mouth though her lips barely moved.

I brushed the white-hot hair from her forehead as she stared at my ceiling. Again she reminded me of a shell, a pink and white conch shell, and I put my ear on her chest to listen for the sea.

One thing I love about the Bay Area is how spring arrives the first of February. That's when the plum and magnolia trees blossom. There you are thinking you're in the dead of winter and suddenly the birds start carrying on like it's spring. Then you realize that it is.

Deirdre Felix called me twice in early February.

Not calling her back ate my insides. I kept picturing her sitting in that big old bus, looking out the rain-streaked window, wearing nothing but wet tennis clothes. Or sitting in the big padded chair reading while the firelight trembled in her study. I could not imagine her not returning a call. I finally decided to get rid of that gnawing feeling by calling her back. I wanted to tell her in words rather than silence that I was quitting the literacy program. I had given it a good three months—mid-September to mid-December—and it just hadn't taken with me. Telling her, woman to woman, was the decent thing to do.

When she answered I said, "This is Lori Taylor," then waited for her to speak.

"Good," she said. "Will this Wednesday night work?"

"I threw away my flash cards."

"Why?"

"I didn't think you'd be calling me again when you said you were going to New York. I mean, I thought our tutoring was over."

I waited to hear her dismissing *pfft.* Instead she sounded a little heated as she said, "I told you I would call when I came back."

When I didn't answer she said, "Never mind about the flash cards. I like fresh starts."

I smiled in spite of my intentions. So did I.

"Wednesday," she said, "six-thirty."

"Sharp," I added.

After I hung up I called Edith to cancel our Wednesday night February the twentieth date. "Edith?" I told her answering machine. "This is Lori. I'm really sorry but something has come up for Wednesday night and I'll have to reschedule. I'd really love to see you though. What about May fifth? Give me a call."

13

A MONTH LATER I TOLD my tape player, "Since Deirdre Felix got back from New York we almost always do the same thing every week. I try to read something for like fifteen minutes, then she gives up and just reads out loud to me.

"What's different is that I've started listening to her read, though I pretend I'm not so she won't ask me comprehension questions. As she reads it's like the words form a cage around me. It's that same cage I felt that night in my car with Whitney sitting there in front of Deirdre Felix's house. Except now I feel like a gorilla, this big brute thing, way too big for the cage. All those words crowd me. It's like someone turned on a glaring light and now I see that the world is ninety-nine percent bigger than I had realized. But I'm still living in this cramped space.

"The thing is, even though *she* hasn't said anything about it, I'm beginning to make a tiny bit of progress. There's a pile of flash cards that I don't have to review anymore because I know them cold. I think I'm a little better at sounding out words too.

Especially if I relax. The problem is I can't seem to remember the words after I've sounded them out even if they show up again a few sentences later. Also, when I'm really concentrating on reading the words I don't remember anything about the content. Piss poor comprehension. As far as Deirdre Felix is concerned I'm still pretty much an F student."

I punched the machine off, then punched it back on for my closing remarks, which had become my mantra, like a prayer: "I miss Mickey."

That night Whitney and I sat outside and enjoyed the unseasonably warm spring evening. The climbing rose was climbing all over my cottage, its sunny buds bursting, and I remembered how Whitney had said she wanted to see it in bloom and how I had been sure she wouldn't. Here she was sitting in my landlady's Adirondack chairs with me, breathing this sweet spring air that smelled like vanilla.

"That's the jasmine," Whitney said.

"Yeah I know," I lied. "Look. Remember you wanted to see the roses in bloom. They're about ready to do it."

"You didn't want me to," she said.

"You knew that?"

"You weren't exactly subtle in your resistance to me."

"I guess not."

"And what do you think now?"

"I let you keep your toothbrush here, don't I?"

She smiled.

"Wait a second," I said, going into my cottage. I came back with a book of poetry Deirdre Felix had read to me and handed it to Whitney. "Read one of these."

"Now?" she asked.

"Yeah."

"Out loud?"

"Why not?"

"I didn't know you read poetry," Whitney said and I could tell she was pleased. "Mary TallMountain. I've never heard of her."

"You haven't? She's an Athabascan poet. Native. Read the one about the wolf." I sounded wonderfully knowledgeable, thanks to Deirdre Felix.

I closed my eyes as Whitney started to read. This was an experiment. Here where the yellow roses climbed all over my cottage, where the jasmine sweetened the night air, where there was lots of space, I wanted to find out what listening to poetry was like.

Whitney didn't read nearly as nicely as Deirdre Felix. She read flatly, but in a way, that was better. I didn't get lulled away from the words. Lately I had been noticing something else about reading, something other than the uncomfortable cage it formed around me, which was that I liked the *sounds* of words, especially the way Deirdre Felix read. You could listen to them almost like you listen to music. Not that boy sailing book, but writers like Mary TallMountain and others Deirdre Felix had read to me.

"You read one now," Whitney said, handing me the book.

I turned it over in my hands a couple of times, then flipped through a few pages like Deirdre Felix did, as if I were studying the poem titles. I did not get that hummingbird feeling in my chest. I did not see flashing lights on the page. I saw words. Just words.

"I'm hungry," I said, shutting the book. "I just wanted to share these poems with you." I'm so cheap—those were the exact words Deirdre Felix had used with me.

"Want to go out for a burrito?"

"No," Whitney said, getting up and coming over to straddle me in the Adirondack chair. I was not positive my landlady was out of town but after a couple of minutes I forgot to worry about it. Whitney and I made love in the jasmine air next to the thorned yellow roses, right there in the Adirondack chair and, later, on the patio cement.

~

Our first fight was mild. On the surface anyway.

Whitney asked, "Why do you avoid seeing me on Wednesday nights?"

Whoa, I thought but only said, "Do I?"

"You do."

"Oh."

"You avoid Wednesday nights and you avoid BONG meetings."

"The BONG meetings are once a month, so if I'm busy that one night—"

"You've been busy that one night for months."

"Maybe I'm not interested in BONG meetings."

"Maybe you're not interested in opening a bike shop."

"Maybe you're more interested in the bike shop than you are in me."

That slowed her down for a moment. Then, "That's not true." Long pause. "You were so high about it that night at the BONG meeting. I hate seeing you give up on your dream."

It was Mickey's dream, not mine, but I said, "Who's giving up?"

"You're not working on it."

When I didn't answer, she said, "What do you do on Wednesday nights?"

"I fuck my brains out with a girlfriend I keep on the side."

"You're not funny."

"What do you want me to say?"

"The truth."

"I don't have to report my hourly schedule to you."

She looked like a sea anemone I had just prodded with a stick.

"Whitney," I said and tried to kiss her.

She turned away. "I don't know, Lori. You keep such a big part of yourself private. Even secret."

I tried to kiss her again. "But don't we have great sex anyway?"

A tiny smile.

"Don't we?"

"Yes."

"Well then." Finally she let me kiss her. In due time, I thought as I slid her belt from the loops, in due time I'd tell her everything.

"Is this you?" I picked up a small framed photo from Deirdre Felix's mantle. A young woman with full cheeks wearing a black evening gown sat with her legs spread and a cello tucked between them. Three young men, two with violins and the third with a bass, stood behind her in the picture. They wore thin fifties-style ties.

"Yes."

"Who are the guys?"

Deirdre Felix picked up the book she'd chosen to read from this week and opened it, flipping past the first pages until she came to the start of the story. I held my ground, did not set the photo back on the mantle, did not sit down to listen. I studied the picture more closely, waiting. Deirdre Felix's eyes were melting in the picture, a young, more intense version of that look she sometimes got as she read to me.

"That's Arnie, the tall violinist."

I nodded without looking up, hoping she'd go on.

"Our college string quartet."

In the picture her head was inclined toward the tall violinist.

"Violinist's hands." She might have been speaking to herself. She pressed her own hand along the crease of the book and said, "Ready?"

I said, "I guess," and she read.

Later that evening as I was leaving her house, Deirdre Felix walked me out the door and down the flagstone path. Huge white blossoms shaped like musical instruments hung from shiny green plants and tiny purple blossoms covered the ground. Though they were lovely, I tried not to look at any of the plants for too long for fear she would have me look them up in the library.

I heard classical music, again, floating out of an upstairs window.

"I have an extra ticket for the ballet tomorrow night," she said. "I wondered if you'd enjoy going."

Oh weird, I thought. Do I look like I would enjoy the ballet? Then I thought how Whitney would be impressed if I told her I had gone to the ballet, so I said, "Okay."

"Why don't you meet me here at seven."

"You mean you're going too?"

Deirdre Felix laughed. "Yes."

I thought she meant she had an extra ticket she couldn't use. She had been so businesslike all these months. Why all of a sudden did she want me to go to the ballet with her? Was this like a *My Fair Lady* thing? Did she think it was part of her job to introduce me to culture? That kind of pissed me off. Besides, what would we talk about?

"I forgot I had a date," I told her.

Deirdre Felix looked embarrassed. I realized how rude I had just been: I would take the ticket but I would not go with her.

"Well, I'm not going alone," she said as if settling something with herself. "I'd be happy if you and your date used the tickets. If you want. I'm not trying to force anything on you. I think you'd enjoy it though. This is the off-season, of course, when they do less traditional work." She smiled and I noticed the little spray of wrinkles shooting out from the corners of her eyes.

"You love the ballet," I said. "You shouldn't miss it."

"*Pfft.*" She waved the ballet away.

"I don't really have a date," I admitted. "Why don't I go with you? I just got nervous."

She stared at me for a moment, obviously irritated, then said with a sigh, "You'll grow out of it."

"Out of what?"

"Taking everything so seriously. The ballet won't hurt you. You might even like it."

I almost snarled something about her being patronizing but figured she was just retaliating for my being so rude. "Okay, okay," I said. "Seven o'clock tomorrow night. I'll meet you here."

As I drove home I remembered that I really did have something I was supposed to do tomorrow night. I did have a date with Whitney after all, one that she would not appreciate my canceling.

Deirdre Felix wore a purple silk pantsuit with a white blouse. She looked nice, especially compared to the other women at Davies Hall who wore furs, silver lamé gowns, I swear I even saw one woman wearing a tiara. "You didn't tell me Lady Di would be here," I whispered to Deirdre Felix and she laughed out loud. I had on my best pants, black chinos, and a silky-looking polyester shirt from the seventies. The pointed collar, about six inches long, was nearly in style again but not in this crowd. Deirdre Felix knew some people and she introduced me as her friend. I had permanent bike grease under my fingernails so I just nodded and said "pleased to meet you" and pretended I did not notice their extended hands.

"Here's your program," she said, handing me a folded piece of paper as we took our seats. I held it carefully.

"Arnie on a business trip?" I asked, petting the burgundy velvet upholstery on the arm of my chair.

"No."

"I guess doctors don't go on business trips," I said, trying to extend the conversation.

She was silent. I sighed loud enough for her to hear. I happened to have gotten myself into deep trouble in order to escort her to the ballet. Maybe she didn't think of it as me escorting her but she didn't have to be so uncommunicative.

Soon the lights went down and the orchestra launched into the first number. I had seen ballet on television, but I had never been to a live dance performance. I expected to see feather-weight femmes in tutus with gayboys carrying them around the stage, but for the first number the dancers wore street clothes, sharp nineteen-forties suits and dresses, and the men danced as much if not more than the women. Their movements were so fluid, so sensual, watching them made me feel as if a rip tide were sucking me under the surface. I knew I would want to tell Whitney all about this, but because of the way I had broken our date I was not going to be able to brag about having been at the ballet.

She had been displeased to say the least. We had plans to go with Joy from Oberlin and her girlfriend to a movie. I had resisted hanging out with Joy or any of Whitney's other friends. I guess I had been sort of afraid of them, so my agreeing to that movie date had been a big deal. Which was probably why I blanked out on it when I told Deirdre Felix I could go to the ballet.

I don't know why I hadn't told Whitney that a cousin of my mother's had come to town unexpectedly, something excusable like that. When it came to Deirdre Felix I just couldn't lie. The best I could do was tell Whitney "something important came up" which sounded suspicious at best. I planned to tell Whitney about Deirdre Felix and the literacy program. Eventually. Even soon. On good days I looked forward to it. I even fantasized how Whitney could help me with my lessons. I needed a little more time though. I would tell her but not yet.

The dancers flew onto the stage in sweats for the second piece, which was my favorite, and in army fatigues for the third one. They told stories with their bodies, whole stories about blood, muscle, sweat, heat. I sat gripping the program with both hands, feeling as if my own blood was sloshing in unison with their movements. The dancers gave me a deep kind of knowledge, a very new and very old kind of knowledge, one I felt vibrating in my whole body, even my little toes.

By the time we left Davies Hall I was skin filled with helium. Deirdre Felix walked slowly like she was tired, but I had trouble keeping my feet on the ground. I opened the car door for her, as I had quit doing for practical Whitney, and Deirdre Felix smiled and said, "Thank you."

When we got out of the car at her house, I wanted to hug her before getting into my own car and driving home. I didn't know what it was but it was there, the way I felt sometimes in her study where she loosened, became someone other than my teacher, as she read stories out loud. I did not hug her. Even if I'd had the nerve I didn't have the time. She shot into her house.

When I got home I put the ballet program on the floor next to my bed. I had made sure not to fold or wrinkle it. I bet she would have me read the program at our next meeting, that was the kind of thing she did. The thing was, I wanted to read it.

However, Deirdre Felix did not have me read the ballet program at our next meeting. In fact, she did not want *me* to read anything at all that week. After we got comfortable in her study she began reading out loud right away. I was disappointed. My progress was nothing to her, a handful of words, but it had begun to feel significant to me. I wanted to try reading the ballet program.

"This book is called *Written on the Body*," she said. "It's by Jeanette Winterson. She's another lesbian author. British. Very different from Rita Mae Brown." She had just finished reading me *Rubyfruit Jungle,* which I loved.

There was no fire this week, hadn't been in a while. These days Deirdre Felix usually opened the window onto her garden where I could watch hummingbirds, some with glossy ruby throats and others with green satin backs, hovering over her flowers.

"You don't mind reading lesbian authors?" I asked.

"Why should I mind?"

"Some people are homophobic."

"*Pfft.*" She shrugged as if she had about a hundred more important things to think about than homophobia. I laughed out loud, liking Deirdre Felix and wanting to ask what were those other things she thought about. I had that feeling again of wanting to sit closer to her. I even had begun liking this intense study. It was as if every atom packed a bigger whollop than atoms anywhere else. When I was in Deirdre Felix's study I longed for the most unusual things. Like wanting to sit close to this woman who was better than twice my age, my teacher. Like actually wondering what stories the other books, the ones she was not reading to me, told.

She began reading from the Jeanette Winterson book, "'Why is the measure of love loss?

"'It hasn't rained for three months. The trees are prospecting underground, sending reserves of roots into the dry ground, roots like razors to open any artery waterfat.'"

A breeze came in the window reminding me of that day at the coast last fall when I had seen the artichoke plant and peregrine falcon. The words Deirdre Felix read seemed to get lifted on the breeze and carried out the window. They had an energy, those words, like the dancers' bodies, a flow, a swishing. And I thought: I am learning to read. No one knew but me, not even Deirdre Felix, but I realized in that moment that I really was learning. Reading was not words and books. It was movement, rhythm. Waves of energy between me and the world. Like a breeze or a dancer. The words and the books were just the working parts.

Deirdre Felix read as if I weren't there, as if reading were a journey. I wondered which she loved most, books or ballet. When she finally finished she shut the book and put it on the table. "Did you enjoy the ballet?" she asked.

I flushed. I had not thanked her. Inside I was still soaring and yet I had not told her. "Yes," I said. "It was great. Really cool. I liked it a lot." All the words, about the breeze, the dancers, books and energy, backed up in my throat. "It's kind of like repairing bikes," I tried. She looked quizzical and I couldn't explain, so I left quickly, too excited to stay.

I drove straight to Mickey's. I pounded on his door, waited about three seconds, then pounded some more. I knew he was in there because his truck was out front. Finally I flipped through the keys on my key ring looking for the one to his apartment that he had once given me so I could feed his cat while he was out of town.

"Hey!" Mickey shouted from the bedroom as I entered the apartment. "Who is it?" He sounded panicked.

"Mickey," I yelled. "It's me. I didn't think you were home," I lied.

"What are you doing?" he demanded, coming from the bedroom, shirtless, barefoot and wearing jeans with the fly open. "Who said you could just break into my apartment?"

I had never seen the long ragged scar just above his left nipple. Sheila trailed out of the bedroom with that same flower print dress pulled on crooked. Mickey collapsed in a kitchen chair. "Damn it, Lori."

I looked at Sheila and wondered again if her parents knew where she was. She moved behind Mickey, placed a hand on his thin shoulder. One finger stroked his skin. "I better go home," she said.

"No," Mickey said to her, then asked me, "What do you want?"

"Listen to this," I said, undaunted by his displeasure in seeing me, his fear, Sheila's presence. I opened a cupboard and pulled out a can of soup. "Okay watch," I said, feeling like a magician. "Camp-bell's," I sounded out slowly, not unlike Charles. "To-ma-to." I giggled, dropped the soup can and grabbed the T-shirt tossed on a kitchen chair. I held it up and read, "'Just do it.' Shit, that one's easy. Give me another."

Mickey was looking at me like I was crazy.

"You don't understand, Mick. I'm getting it. Decoding words is just like repairing a bike: You take the parts apart and then you figure out how they go back together again. And then, *then* you have the *ride!*" I found a tissue box and started in on it. "In-tro-ducing a nnnew sof-sof-ter tis-sue. Introducing a new softer tissue! Do you hear me, Mickey! Do you get it?"

"Who is this, Miguel?" Sheila asked.

Mickey—or I guess he was Miguel now, at least to Sheila—wiped his face with both hands. "It's Lori," he said. "My coworker."

"I'm his best friend," I told the girl. "He's forgotten. Believe me, he'll remember one day."

Now Mickey looked directly at me and he had a double expression on his face. I could see he wanted me gone, instantly, but a feeling of responsibility, maybe even caring, nagged behind his aggravation, enough to make him say, "Okay, Lori. That's great. You can read the soup can."

"And the T-shirt. And the tissue box. I'm saying I'm learning to read. I can't *read* read but I *get* it. I get the *feeling* of reading. It's rhythm, like music. Energy, like dance!" I must have looked psycho. My synapses were snapping and popping like I had just inhaled a couple hits of acid.

Sheila slipped out the door and Mickey said, "Shit. She can't walk home alone at night." He pulled on the 'Just do it' T-shirt, grabbed his keys off the coffee table and chased after her. He yelled, "Lock up when you leave."

"Zip up your fly," I called after him.

Naturally I would have liked a little more attention from Mickey but mostly I had needed a witness. To make myself believe it. I locked up his apartment and drove home fast. When I got there I opened the tiny fridge and read the tortilla package. I pulled off the T-shirt I wore and read the label. I read the little tag hanging off the electrical cord on my blow dryer. I looked at an envelope from the DMV sitting on the counter, tore it open and looked at the jumble of words.

That stopped me. The hummingbird came back. I could not read anything in that letter. It was too black and white, too long.

I opened my cottage door and breathed in the vanilla jasmine. The air was cold now, cold and dark. I sat in one of the Adirondack chairs wearing just my bra and jeans, and wondered if Deirdre Felix had gone to bed or if she was up reading. I imagined her reading and reading and reading all night long. When she wasn't with me or at the ballet I thought she read. I took another deep breath and realized I was still holding the letter from the DMV.

I thought of the dancers. I thought of her garden. I thought of Mary TallMountain and Rita Mae Brown and Jeanette Winterson. The way their words sang. I thought again of Deirdre Felix and knew she had become as essential to me as air.

14

DEIRDRE FELIX INVITED ME to the ballet again a few weeks later. I still had not found a way to tell her what I had been trying to tell Mickey, though I rehearsed versions of the telling time and again. I went out the afternoon of the ballet and bought a pair of loose pants made of an orange, black and tan African print, a nice black silk blouse, a loose tan linen vest and some decent looking black loafers.

As we took our seats in Davies Hall, I noticed that Deirdre Felix was not wearing her big diamond ring that night and I felt a surge of protectiveness toward her. She looked terrible, red-eyed and rough-skinned, and I was certain she was going through something big and painful. Lately, the soft pockets of skin under her eyes were plumped out more often than not and she had developed a habit of tapping one of her fingers, as she was doing now on her purse. Sometimes she did it really hard. It reminded me of someone trying not to cry. I was glad we were at the ballet because she loved it so much.

As we sat and waited for the performance to begin, I searched for conversation. Her missing ring as well as the orchestra tuning up a few feet in front of us must have led me to say, "So you met Arnie playing in the college quartet."

My unfortunate choice of comment jarred like a wrong note. She nodded yes.

"Then what?" I asked, my curiosity getting the best of me. What the hell, I thought, she doesn't have to answer.

"Medical school for Arnie. Housekeeping for me." She smirked.

"You didn't want to be a housewife?"

"Oh I wanted to be a housewife very much. Arnie didn't want to be a doctor."

"He didn't?"

"He wanted to be a professional musician."

"Why didn't he do that?"

Deirdre Felix rubbed her fingers up and down the shiny leather of her purse. Her nostrils flared gently and her eyebrows hopped twice. "Musicians are like ventriloquists. They speak through their music. You never know if it's the person speaking or something else. Someone else."

"Oh." She'd lost me, so I opened my program and tried to read some of the words.

Deirdre Felix sat and tapped.

Finally the ballet began. Halfway through the first piece I looked at Deirdre Felix. Her eyebrows were slightly raised and her eyes shiny with tears. She had quit tapping her finger. I looked away quickly but she had been too mesmerized by the performance to notice me staring.

It struck me then how many different kinds of things can move a person and how being moved is what counts, not what moves you. And how the more deeply you are moved, the harder it is to define what it is that is doing the moving. The dancers moved me. Deirdre Felix moved me deeply. Why? Was I in love with her? I think it was something very much bigger than being in love. It was her books, no not just the paper and ink but the room of stories in which she lived, her study, and the dancers she loved, her generosity to me. Not generosity of time, and certainly not of words, but of spirit.

I absorbed as much of the ballet as I could, every twitch of muscle, flick of sweaty hair, even the tiny grunts we could occasionally hear from our seats. I tried to figure out the story of each dance, but also the real stories of the dancers' lives. Who was in love with whom? Were all the men gay? Were all the women straight? How old were they and did they have to think about every morsel of food they put in their mouths? Did they love their lives as dancers or was it grueling?

Afterwards Deirdre Felix suggested we go out for a drink.

A drink! With Deirdre Felix! As much as I wanted to know everything about her I had become attached to our formality. The starch of our relationship had a certain dignity. How dare she suggest we share something as mundane as a drink! She and I, we read books and shared art.

Of course I went anyway.

At Max's on Opera Plaza I ordered a whiskey sour thinking that was the kind of drink you had after the ballet. She ordered a martini and asked the waitress for a pack of cigarettes. Holding a lit cigarette made her look like shit, like she hadn't slept in weeks.

"I didn't know you smoked."

"I don't. Or I hadn't in about forty years until a couple of weeks ago. Do you mind if I do now?"

I shook my head no, thought yes.

She inhaled deeply on the cigarette, breathed out the smoke and said, "You're a courageous woman, Lori."

I stared blankly. Me?

"Yes you," she said as if I had spoken my question out loud. She took another long pull on the cigarette. "Living openly as a lesbian. Facing your reading disability head on. I want you to know that I've gotten a great deal out of spending time with you."

"You have?" My voice a mere wheeze.

Deirdre Felix smiled that off-hand smile of hers. She tossed back her gray hair and blew smoke out of puckered lips into the air above her head. "My husband is seeing another woman. A much younger woman. That might not mean a lot to you. It shouldn't mean so much to me. He's had other affairs but this one he's having in public. And she's twenty-five. Some secretarial floozy." She laughed. "Of course for her it's his money." She paused, then said, "Well, Arnie *is* handsome." She made that puffing sound with her lips and waved some smoke away from our table, then shook her head slightly, like she couldn't believe she was in this situation.

"He's an asshole," I blurted. "And a fool."

She exhaled with a small grunt of laughter. "He *is* an asshole. But no fool."

I felt furious.

"You asked me what happened after the string quartet." She gave her full attention to her cigarette for a moment. Then, "He was the one with the vision. All I wanted was the 1950s thing, babies and a big house. I joined his parents in pushing him into medical school." Her words sounded like metal filings. "In a way I made Arnie into the stereotype he's become."

"No one can make anybody something else."

"That's true. But if the person you love pushes against you, along with everyone else in the world, that's the worst kind of betrayal."

"But no one can blame someone else for—"

She waved her hand through the air to cut me off.

"The big joke," she said after a silence that lasted much longer than I'm comfortable with, "is that I still love the Arnie in that photo, the one I so stubbornly opposed, and I don't even know the Arnie I live with today."

I didn't dare say anything.

"Anyway Lori, I'm a complete wreck. As much as I draw strength from your courage, I need to stop tutoring. I'm filing for divorce and I'm just too overwhelmed. I want you to get a new tutor. You deserve a lot better than I can do right now."

I reached for the pack of cigarettes. She beat me to it and stuffed the pack in her purse. "You don't smoke," she said.

"Neither do you."

"Did you hear what I just told you?"

"I'll wait. Until your divorce goes through and you're settled down."

"No, please," she said a little desperately. "I need time. Lots of time."

I took a swallow of my whiskey sour and swished the tangy sweetness of it around in my mouth. I waited for the word *no* to quit bouncing off the walls of my head. I asked, "What happened that time someone dropped you off at the library? You were wearing your tennis clothes."

She was silent. Her eyes looked hot and dry.

"Was that Arnie driving the tan BMW?"

"Yes."

"You were really upset."

Deirdre Felix pulverized the burning end of her cigarette in the ashtray as she said, "Arnie totaled my Saab that morning. The girl was in the car with him. That's how I found out about her. Unfortunately neither of them suffered so much as a scratch. Starting that evening, and for a couple of days after, I made him drive me around to my appointments." She found the pack in her purse and pulled out another cigarette. "As if that were the point. As if my car were the point."

She lit the cigarette and I reached over and took it out of her hand. I put it out in the ashtray. She didn't object or even comment. I hated Arnie.

"I need to go home," she said.

On the drive back to Oakland I chatted about work and Mickey, casually, like her quitting was no big deal, like replacing a tutor was the same as getting a new bike, something you had to get used to, nothing more. She drove fast and it felt as if she were trying to get me home, rid of me, as soon as possible. As we flew across the Bay Bridge I tried to accelerate the conversation, which was really just me talking, to get her attention, make her change her mind.

I said, "You know it occurred to me recently that maybe my father can't read either. I asked my mother last week but she just changed the subject. They're like divorced and everything but I guess she still covers for him, know what I mean? It's a habit. Besides, my mother doesn't exactly want to acknowledge that *I* can't read. Anyhow I'm thinking that's why Dad always stood up for me."

I was babbling. Why did I mention divorce?

It was just that I had wanted to tell Deirdre Felix all of this. I had wanted to tell her about the soup can, the tortilla package, Mickey's "Just Do It" T-shirt, what I had realized about words and books being the working parts and stories being the ride. I had thought I had time.

I said, "I was always really grateful for my father's defense. But now. I don't know. I think he hurt me by expecting so little."

What I wanted to say and couldn't was this: The way I annoyed her when I didn't try or got sarcastic, the way she expected so much of me, made me want to worship at her feet.

"Good night," she said, yanking on the parking brake in her driveway. I got out of her car and walked to my own in the street while she charged up the flagstone path and disappeared into her house. I stood in the dark beside my car for a few seconds feeling more inadequate than I had ever felt in my life. Which was saying a lot.

Lying in bed that night all I could think was that I had failed. If I had improved in those seven months I'd been in the program, even a little bit, I could have kept Deirdre Felix. I might have made her feel good about being such a good tutor. All this time I had been only a distraction for her, a way not to think about her husband dumping her for a babe. I pictured that blonde in the slinky blue dress, surely she was the secretarial floozy. I heard the rough,

122

I'm-in-control-of-everything voice of Arnie, it must have been him, calling into the woods behind his house. Deirdre Felix had tutored me so that she could get away from that blue body, that virile voice. Basically she had used me. Which in a strange way comforted me. It implied her need. Our mutual need. But what, besides distraction, had I given her?

At four in the morning I got out of bed. I opened my cottage door. I breathed the air, now only faintly tickled by a lingering jasmine scent. I shut the door again and collected my flash cards. I sat on my bed and flipped through them looking for words. When I found ones I wanted, I put them aside. Then I spent the next three hours working on this poem.

> *I am like a peregrine falcon*
> *the way I dive and miss,*
> *dive and miss.*
> *But this time I caught something.*
>
> *You are like a wild artichoke*
> *prickly and elegent*
> *on the outside.*
> *But your heart is rich and complex.*

At seven-thirty I called Mickey and he actually answered. "Mick, how do you spell 'elegant'?" He told me. "What about 'prickly'?" He rattled off those letters too. "How'd you get so smart?" I asked him. "See you in a few."

On the way to work I swung by the post office and mailed the poem to Deirdre Felix. By the time I reached the shop I regretted it. I called the post office and asked if there was a way to retrieve a letter. "I'd pay anything," I told the lady.

"Sorry miss. You mailed it, we'll deliver it."

I said, "What if I mailed a bomb?"

The lady said, "Are you saying that? Because if you are we'd be contacting the FBI pronto."

"No," I reassured her. "I'm not saying that. There's no bomb." I hung up quickly before she could trace the call. A bomb wasn't a bad idea though. I could find out where Arnie's office was and level it.

After work that afternoon I turned on my tape player. I rewound the tape to a week before, pressed "play" and heard myself say, "When I listen to Deirdre Felix read I think about what it must feel like to have read all those books in her study. It's like her head is a fire and books are logs. The thing is, I can feel that fire in my own head. Well maybe it's just a spark. But here's the truth: I am going to learn to read. I think I really am. Lori Taylor is literate. Ha!" I had laughed into the tape machine like an idiot.

I fast-forwarded to the blank part of the tape, pushed "record" and said, "May thirtieth. *Hardly* literate. Like in the seven months I worked with her I learned maybe fifty new words. That's not even ten a month. My comprehension is still shit." I turned off the machine.

I wished I were seeing Whitney alone tonight. We were going to El Rio with Joy from Oberlin and her girlfriend Sue to hear some hot new lesbo punk band. To make up for my canceling that first date with them I had agreed to several evenings with her friends *and* promised to attend the next BONG meeting. Actually I liked Joy and especially Sue, who had the most amazing cloud of frizzy red hair and a great sense of humor. Sue and I liked to see how long a string of jokes we could crack without taking a break and also how fast we could annoy the more serious-minded Oberlin graduates.

Tonight though I didn't know if I could handle humor or Oberlin. I had slept all of two hours the night before and sincerely wished I had not sent that dumb poem. I had just wanted to give something back to Deirdre Felix but why did I think she would want a poem from me?

I put on baggy jeans and a white T-shirt. I tied on some neon yellow Converse hightops and looked at myself in the mirror. My hair was pulled back in a loose ponytail, not very exciting. I wished Whitney and I could just stay at her apartment and have sex. I needed a break from my thoughts, I needed deliverance from myself.

I locked up my cottage and instead of going straight to Whitney's, I drove up Tunnel Road and out Skyline. Just as I rolled to a stop in front of her house the BMW backed out of the driveway. My whole body flashed hot. I didn't wait to see who was driving the car. I hit the gas and shot out of there.

I was fifteen minutes late and brimming with confused feelings about Deirdre Felix by the time I picked up Whitney.

"My mom has this cousin who lives in town," I told Whitney as we drove across the Bay Bridge. "And she—"

"You never told me that."

"It wasn't important. Anyway I talked to her this week and found out she's getting a divorce."

"Do you see her often?"

"Occasionally."

"Why is she getting a divorce?"

"Her husband is having an affair with some secretarial floozy."

"When you associate the words 'secretarial' and 'floozy' like that you make it sound like they always go together, like secretaries are necessarily dumb."

"Those were her words."

"You don't have to repeat them."

"Okay, I just feel bad for . . . my mom's cousin."

"Does your mom's cousin have a name?"

"Deirdre Felix," I said and felt a wave of comfort, as if I had begun telling the truth.

"I had an interview for that job."

"What job?" I asked, annoyed at Whitney for changing the subject.

"The one I told you about a couple of months ago. With that graphics firm."

125

"But you said you weren't interested."

"I figured it can't hurt to do the interview."

"I don't get it. You're obsessed with me starting my business and you're getting ready to give yours up."

"No one's giving up," she said. "Whose house are we staying at tonight?"

"I don't know. Why?"

"I just wondered." She snuggled over next to me in the front seat. "Sometimes I get tired of always feeling like I'm camping out."

"Meaning?"

"I wish one of us wasn't always not at home."

If that wasn't the beginning of a let's-move-in-together talk, I didn't know what it was. I felt confused by the pace of the conversation: from my lies about Deirdre Felix to Whitney's job interview to her hints about living together. My heart felt like a suck hole with white water swirling around the perimeter. I saw Whitney there on the edges about to get washed into the center.

We didn't talk anymore but Whitney touched me—my ribs, the rim of my ear, the inside of my knee—while I drove. She was masterful at sexual subtlety and her touch always soothed and excited me at the same time, a deliciously absorbing combination. By the time we reached El Rio in the Mission District, I felt only the full heat of my body and was no longer thinking about Deirdre Felix quitting me or about the poem I sent her. We bought beer and headed for the patio. Sue, the girlfriend with the big red frizz, greeted me with a high five and we started joking around. As I bantered with her and half-listened to Joy and Whitney rehash, oh yet again, their Oberlin years, I looked around El Rio. There was a big crowd tonight to hear the music. I saw Dr. Julie Higginboth, the sex workshop leader, and thought she saw me. I smiled and started to wave as she floated by on her way to greet someone behind me. I turned and watched her tongue-kiss a woman wearing black velour bell bottoms. I cringed at the public display of sexuality. Did that make me sex-negative? I turned

126

to ask Sue but—there was Edith! I felt a moment's joy in seeing my old friend, then remembered the May fifth date and my stomach plummeted. She had entirely missed my sarcasm, called back and said she would love to see me May fifth, that she would make dinner and that I should show up at seven o'clock. That was over three weeks ago. I poured my beer into the soil surrounding a palm and excused myself.

In the bathroom I stood in front of the mirror and looked at my face. I looked for so long that it started to look like someone else's face, like I could only see the separate parts—nose, glasses, cheekbones, lips—not the whole face. Maybe it was sleep deprivation but my life suddenly looked very shaky. First there was Mickey. We had patched things up after the "break-in episode," as he called it, but we had to, we worked together. We still joked around in the shop but it wasn't the same between us, not even close. I may have burned my last bridge with Edith. Pam was a faint memory. And Deirdre Felix just dumped me. What, I asked my reflected face, does it all mean? It was like the me I had always known wasn't there anymore. Who had replaced her?

Just then Whitney pushed through the bathroom door. "There you are. I got worried."

I smiled at her but it was a canned smile, a little loony. "I'm fine."

"The band started," she said. "But they're really loud. We were thinking of leaving, going somewhere we could talk. Sue's hungry."

"Good," I agreed. "Me too. Let's go."

Later that night, driving back across the bridge, I impulsively said, "Maybe you should move in with your toothbrush."

Was I joking? I had to be.

Whitney didn't laugh. She looked out the passenger window, waited a few beats, then said, "What about your Wednesday night mystery dates?"

"I guess they'd have to stop. No more hot babes on the side."

Whitney still didn't laugh. "If we live together," she said, "I want us to be really open with each other. I'm a little scared by the way you get, oh, what is it? Protective of your emotional space."

Whoa. Rules already.

Then she said, "I guess I'm also kind of worried about what Dad would say."

"Your dad," I said. "What does he have to do with anything?"

She jerked around to scowl at me.

I closed my eyes for a second, long enough to veer into the next lane. I pulled the car straight again. I knew I should leave it be, this moving in idea, but I felt a void inside me, made huge by the withdrawal of Deirdre Felix. I felt like a big empty house.

"Just move in," I said. "Do it this weekend."

15

In June I saw Charles, the adult learner, in the grocery store. I stood in one line and he stood in the next one over. He wore the same fine leather jacket he had had on the first time I saw him at the library and some nice dark burgundy dress trousers. He was buying a six-pack of Coke. Though I knew better by now, I could not get over how regular he looked. It was hard to imagine this nice-looking adult sounding out words like a six-year-old. He caught me staring, once, then twice. We paid at the same time and as we walked out the automatic door, him behind me, he spoke roughly, "Do I know you?" Unsaid was, and if I don't why were you staring at me?

"No," I said.

Then he smiled, rolled his head back in recognition and said, "Yeah, I do. The library, right?" I didn't answer but he asked, "How's your tutor? Do you like her?"

"Um—" I started.

"My tutor, Mr. Jackson, that's what he goes by, he's kind of old-fashioned. He's real good people though." I remembered the white-haired African-American gentleman who worked with Charles. He shifted the bag of Coke under one arm and held out his other hand. "I'm Charles." I knew that. Now I had the feeling he felt sorry for me, that he was trying to make me comfortable.

"I'm Lori. Nice to meet you." I shook his hand, then turned with my bag of groceries toward the parking lot.

Charles said, "I haven't seen you at the library in a while."

I stopped, said, "I'm not in the program anymore."

"That's too bad. It's changed my life."

How do you just walk away when someone has said *that?*

"Yeah?" I said noncommittally.

"Yeah." He ran his tongue over his lips thoughtfully and I could tell he was going to deliver a pitch for the program. "I used to work over at the GM plant in Fremont but I got laid off a couple of years ago. A guy I worked with over there was in the program. He talked me into giving it a try. My tutor—Mr. Jackson—helped me fill out job applications. Took me a year to get a job and it's only janitorial, not nearly so good as I had at the plant, but hey, it's a job. I'm gonna get my GED. Got a long way to go, but I'm going." He threw back his head and laughed, a laugh that was all joy. "The best part though is my kids. They see me studying at night and they want to study too."

"I don't have kids," I said.

"It's how I feel." He patted his chest. "In here. Everything seems possible."

Of course I knew what he was talking about. I knew exactly what he was talking about.

"That's great," I said. "Nice meeting you. Gotta fly."

"There's going to be a writing class for new readers at the library later this summer. Come check it out."

"Sure," I said. "Thanks."

I dumped the groceries in my trunk and got in the car. A few parking aisles over I saw Charles start up an old Dodge Dart. I was surprised he didn't hate me after how I'd let my own shame drive him out of the library last fall. Maybe that was why he wanted to tell me his story. He had a lot of heart, I had to give him that. All the way home I saw him pat his chest, look me in the eye, say, "It's how I feel. In here."

I pushed Whitney onto my bed.

"That won't work," she said. "Get dressed."

"It'd make a lot more sense for me to go next month," I argued. "It'd be like motivation. I'll *have* to do something about the business plan so that I can report to the business ladies." I found it impossible to avoid sarcasm just then.

"Motivation is exactly why you're coming now. They'll help you get going. Come on, they all know about procrastination, how scary it is to start a business. Besides, you promised."

I did promise. Still, I had a little different take on humiliation than Whitney. It might be motivation for her but it felt like torture to me. All those bright shining college-educated faces demanding how much money my bike shop had made so far. Well, I would explain, the bike shop is still nonexistent. Somehow that did not feel motivational.

I was wearing jeans and a T-shirt. Whitney told me to put on something "nicer," which irritated me. She started going through my drawers which also irritated me. Since the night at El Rio we had not discussed moving in together, but I noticed that my rash little invitation had been enough to make Whitney much more comfortable in my cottage. She found the African print pants and black silk shirt. She shook out the pants and looked them over approvingly.

"For a meeting?" I asked. Those were my ballet clothes. I put them on anyway and added the tan linen vest.

As I followed her down the path to the street I kept grabbing at her body, trying to be playful but actually being annoying. It was that inner teenager of mine. Whitney walked faster to get away from my hand. In my landlady's front yard, I pushed her against the rough bark of the cedar tree and kissed her. "Lori," Whitney finally laughed, then sighed. "Sweetie, come on. What's with you? Why do you dread this so much?" She looked seriously perplexed and that scared me. I didn't want her delving too deeply into my resistance.

"Do you realize that this is the first time you've told me no," I said, trying to untuck her shirt. "The first time you've not melted under my kisses."

"Lori." She grabbed my wrists.

"Okay let's go." I marched out to the car silently, swearing I would not make love to her for a whole week to punish her, no matter how hard she tried to seduce me.

The meeting was at the house with the white leather couch. Instead of puff pastries there was artichoke heart spread, which reminded me of Deirdre Felix and my horrid poem, and chocolate-dipped strawberries. The plates were small but I loaded one up as full as I could. Whitney looked at my plate and scowled.

Alix, the curly-headed hostess, handed me a glass of wine and I asked if she had any Coke. Now Whitney widened her eyes at me and cocked her head. "There's some bubbly water right there," she said sharply.

Alix put a hand on my arm and said, "That's okay. I have Coke." She returned with a small glass of it. I took a sip and thought of Charles leaving the grocery store with his six-pack of Coke, saw him pat his chest. *How I feel. In here.* How I felt at the moment, *in there,* was pretty crummy. I did not want to be at this meeting.

Then I heard someone say *Rubyfruit Jungle* and I got a little squirt of confidence. I turned and saw that it was Joy. "I've read that," I said.

"Who hasn't," someone laughed. "It's like the dyke primer."

"The Dick and Jane of lesbian reading," Whitney joked.

My hand started to shake and some Coke spilled out of the glass. Whitney glanced down at the white shag carpet. "Missed," I said to her and licked the Coke off my hand.

132

She gave me a stern look.

"How about *Written on the Body?* That's a good one," I offered.

"What, now we're just shouting out the dyke books we've read?" Whitney said and a few women laughed with her.

I held my glass up to Alix and, making sure Whitney heard me, asked, "Is there more Coke?"

Alix brought a whole can and I thanked her. I did not pour it into the wine glass as she had done but drank straight from the can.

"Don't spill," Whitney whispered as we settled onto the white leather couch for the meeting.

"How're ya doin," I said to Dory sitting across from me. I held up my Coke can in greeting.

"So where've you been?" Dory asked with fake enthusiasm. "Too much business to come to the meetings? Tell us everything!"

Everyone looked at me.

All the air got sucked out of the room. I thought of how Whitney wouldn't let me seduce her out of this meeting. I thought of Charles licking his lips, stumbling over easy words. I thought of Deirdre Felix holding a cigarette, telling me she needed time, lots of time. Still they waited for me to speak.

"Pulled in my first million," I said. "We're opening stock to the public. Anyone interested?"

Everyone cracked up, including Whitney, and I could tell she was pleased the group wit was her girlfriend.

She piped up for me, "I think Lori was hoping we'd help her outline the business plan."

I saw a bit of tension slip out of Dory's body, satisfaction settle on her face. No competition from this front.

Whitney pulled a tablet and pen out of her black bag and handed them to me.

"There's no reason I should go first," I said. "This might take a while. Why don't we go around the room. Do everyone else first—"

Alix interrupted me. "I can't speak for the whole group, but I'd

133

love to work on your business plan. That's the hardest part, getting started. Let's give it, say, half an hour? Then we'll have time for other women's business too. Agreed?"

Everyone was.

"I have a suggestion for how to start," Alix continued. "I found this essay by Regina Wallace—she's that Olympic sprinter? It's very motivational. I thought maybe we could read it out loud."

What was with these women and the word "motivational?"

Anything, though, to postpone working on my business plan. I said, "Go for it."

"Would you like to read it?" Alix asked me.

"You read it," I said. "You have a great voice." I said that a little too flirtatiously and one or two of the women laughed nervously. I tried to look cocky.

"We'll all read," Alix said, "taking turns," and she began.

"Excuse me," I interrupted. "How long is it?"

"Just a couple of pages."

She began again. If she passed it to her right there were six women before me. If she passed it to her left there were only two. I hoped she read a lot of it before passing.

After only a couple of sentences Alix passed the book to her left.

"Go that way," I said, pointing to her right.

Most of the women laughed at my "joke" and the one on Alix's left took the book. I ran through my options and did not hear a word that was read. I could get instant diarrhea which would be embarrassing but not as embarrassing as the truth. I couldn't say that I didn't have my glasses because they were on my face. The woman passed the book to Whitney sitting next to me. Whitney read slowly and enunciated each word carefully, just as she had read the Mary TallMountain poem. She stopped after a minute and turned to me, "That last sentence," she said, "seems particularly applicable to your bicycle shop. Don't you think?"

I nodded.

Whitney said, "How would you work out something like that

then? In the context of a bike shop I mean."

I wanted to strangle her. I felt as if someone was strangling me. I saw Charles's face again. I thought of him patting his chest. What would he do now?

He probably would say that he had not listened and that he could not read. He would say it without shame. With dignity. Which was something I did not, at least at the moment, have.

"I don't know," I said.

"Well now," Whitney said gearing up. "Listen to this next sentence."

She read again and I tried to listen but could not. I couldn't hear anything but the blood pounding in my temples. She stopped reading and waited for a response. Joy jumped in with some enthusiastic insight and the group chatted with energy for several minutes. I wouldn't have minded running out of the room, leaving the meeting and never coming back. But Whitney. What could I tell Whitney?

I picked up the Coke can and took a swig. I missed my mouth and a big splash of it landed on my tan vest just as Whitney handed me the book and said, "Your turn."

"Whoops," Joy said, seeing me spill the Coke.

"You're in the hot seat now," Dory said as if she were joking. She was the type who could smell fear a mile away and enjoyed working it.

I passed the book to my left. "Here," I said. "I better go get this Coke off my vest."

I started to stand up but Alix blocked me. She had a sopping cloth in her hand and she pushed me back in my seat. Standing between my open knees she dabbed at the Coke on my vest. "All gone," she said in a sweet voice. The woman on my left passed the book back to me.

"You know," I said. "These are my regular glasses. I don't have my reading glasses with me."

"Reading glasses?" Whitney said. "Since when?"

I sat very still in my wet vest. I tried to sit up straighter. It would be a good time to shut up, to insist with my silence, but with everyone staring at me I could not squelch the urge to keep talking. "I have a sore throat coming on. I'm going to pass on my turn right now."

"No excuses!" Dory said as if she were being playful. "Everyone reads. At least a couple of sentences."

Whitney put her finger on the place where she had stopped reading and said, "Here." She nestled in closer for moral support, as if I were just shy.

I implored Alix, whom I had found to be sensitive, with my eyes. On cue she said, "Why should she read if she has a sore throat? Pass the book."

I started to but Whitney held my arm. I saw that perplexed look on her face again, the one that scared me, but mixed with another look, very teacherly. Later, I would recognize that moment as the time my feelings for her soured. Not because she was embarrassing me but because I felt like a project of hers, an experiment. "Read," she said in the same tone a TV mother would say, "Eat your vegetables." It would be good for me. She would cure me of whatever silly phobia or shyness caused my refusal.

I turned to the other women and said, "It drives me wild when she orders me to read." Then to Whitney, "Honey, not in public." Alix hooted, the others laughed and once again I was the life of the party. They were relieved I had sprung the weird tension Whitney created by trying to force me to read. Whitney was the embarrassed one now. Even so, when I tried to take the book out of her hands, she gripped hard for a second before letting go. I'd made her mad.

As I passed the book to the woman on my left, I smiled, looked at Dory and said, "What if I told you all I didn't know *how* to read?"

I was the joker, so they laughed again, everyone but Whitney, confident that this not very funny remark was nonetheless a joke. One woman held up her notebook and pretended to read in a slow, laborious manner, like she were sounding out words. I waited for her to finish. No one thought she was funny but they laughed anyway. It was the polite thing to do.

Alix said, "Illiteracy is a big problem in our society."

"They say that up to twenty percent of the population can't read."

"You have to distinguish between being illiterate and having English as a second language. A lot of Americans can read in their native tongues, just not in English."

These women seemed to know quite a lot about the topic. Actually they were eager to let one another know what they knew on any topic. I listened, almost enjoying myself now, like I was spying or eavesdropping. It was like listening to straight people talk about queer people when they didn't know they had one for an audience. There's a perverse sense of power in listening to their ignorance. For me too there was the relief in discussing the taboo topic openly, even if I did not come out personally. I have to admit that I learned some things from these women. I hadn't known that twenty percent of Americans couldn't read. Alix said that it was the fucked up education system that caused it. She sounded like my father.

Finally Alix hushed everyone and motioned for the woman on my left to finish reading the motivational passage. The moment I was sure she had read the last word I announced in a firm, assertive voice that I preferred working on my business plan alone. I insisted the group work on someone else's business problem. These women responded well to assertiveness. They moved on. I counted the seconds until the meeting was over.

In the car driving home Whitney was quiet, too quiet. It was a hot night and we had our windows rolled down. The rush of warm air felt like freedom. I missed Deirdre Felix and I filled the silence by talking about her, how she loved the ballet, how she inhaled books like they were food, but reverently, like they were gourmet food, how she lived in an art-filled house.

"Why do you talk about your mother's cousin so much?" Whitney asked. "You're obsessed with her."

"I am not."

"Is she who you used to see on Wednesday nights?"

I thought about that one for a minute, then said, "Yes."

"You didn't start talking about her until you quit seeing her. Now you talk about her constantly. What's going on, Lori?"

"She's just this woman—"

"How old is this woman?"

"Twenty-five and gorgeous," I said sarcastically. I reached for Whitney's hand but she would not let me have it. "For god's sake she's an old lady, like seventy or something. Why do you care if I like my mom's cousin?"

"How often do you see her?"

"I don't anymore."

"Why not?"

"I told you, she's getting a divorce."

Whitney pulled into herself like a turtle. She took a deep breath and said, "You acted kind of foolishly at the meeting."

"What do you mean? I thought we were talking about Deirdre Felix."

"Refusing to read. Cracking all those dumb jokes."

"Everyone else was amused. *Alix* was amused."

"That's because you were flirting with her."

I parked in front of Whitney's apartment building. I pulled the parking brake and started to get out of the car.

"Lori," Whitney said, stopping me. "You don't have reading glasses. You don't have a sore throat."

I looked out the car window. The apartment building in which Whitney lived was on a busy street. I watched the cars fly by, hot metal on hot rubber rolling on hot pavement. I turned back to Whitney. Her skin looked cool, creamy and cool.

"Have you given any more thought to moving in?" I asked, throwing my whole life up as a decoy. "We could find a bigger place."

She waited.

"Well?" I said.

"Lori."

"What?"

"Who's Deirdre Felix?"

"She was my tutor."

"Tutor?"

"Yeah."

"Like in college?"

And I thought I was the dumb one.

I looked out on the street, my face framed by the car window, and let the hot carbon monoxide-laden air blast my face. The fumes tasted good tonight, rich and oily, deadly.

"No," I said. "In the Literacy Project at the library."

"What?"

A lightning bolt of sarcasm lit me, then another of anger, but they moved so fast I didn't have time to speak them. I slumped, feeling suddenly very fatigued, and repeated, "In the Literacy Project at the library."

"You really can't read?" She was incredulous.

"I can read some."

"How much?"

Now *I* was incredulous. "Does that matter? I mean to us? Now?"

Whitney's hands gripped her black bag.

"I wanted to tell you. I was scared. It doesn't change anything. I'm not in the program anymore," I said as if that would help. "We can talk about all of this later. Are you ready to go in?"

Whitney shook her head. "No wait. I don't understand."

"What's not to understand?"

"How did you graduate from Cal if you can't read?"

"I didn't say I *graduated* from Cal. I said I'd gone there."

"You lied?"

My hands involuntarily flew up in front of my chest, like she'd pulled a gun out of her bag. I placed them on the steering wheel. "I wouldn't call it a lie."

"Oh? What would you call it?" Whitney flushed so red her

white-blond eyebrows looked like flashes of light.

I remembered the conversation. Whitney had asked where I had gone to school. I named my high school. She laughed, said she meant college. I mumbled that I had gone to Cal, purposely saying it that way because I had sometimes gone there for events. Of course I knew she would take it to mean I had graduated from there. Next she had asked my major and I said science. *Science,* she laughed. Just *science?* Physics? Chemistry? Environmental? Biology? Exasperated, she rattled off about thirty options. I said physics because that was what Mickey had studied at the junior college. Whitney liked that answer, said it was appropriate for someone opening a bike shop, though she added it was too bad I didn't have a business background. Then she talked about a class she had taken at Oberlin called "Physics for Poets." She had learned that time travel might one day be possible as physicists learned more about black holes. Mickey had told me lots about this topic and I was able to tell her things she didn't know. The tension from my saying I majored in "science" disappeared. I gained confidence over the months that she didn't know jack about physics. Sometimes I would tell her things Mickey had told me and score points.

The jig was up now.

"I'm sorry," I said.

"What else have you lied about?"

"Nothing. Nothing else. You have no idea," I told her, my throat scratching the words, "how hard this is. How this feels."

She batted her eyes furiously. She was past reason, past compassion. It was as if my confession tripped her own darkest fear.

"I was scared to tell you," I said. Then I tried for a joke, "And here you thought I had some other woman on Wednesday nights."

"I knew you didn't have another woman."

"We'll talk," I said. "We'll talk all about it."

"Okay."

"Ready to go in?"

"I don't care that you can't read," she said.

140

Now who was the liar?

"It's that you made stuff up. About college."

"That's the only thing I made up."

"Lied about," she whispered.

Later, I'd wonder why I didn't say, *Fuck you, get out of the car.* It was that gaping hole in me, the emptiness that felt like desperation. It was how when we touched I was tricked into believing she could fill the emptiness.

I opened my car door. "Let's go in. We can talk some more inside."

"I need a little time alone," she said.

That had always been my line. I said, "No problem. Fine. I'll see you on Saturday then. We're biking, right?"

"Yeah."

"Okay, sweetie," I said using her word, pretending I didn't feel foolish. "I'll talk to you soon."

She got out of the car and I watched her climb the apartment building steps. She didn't turn and wave like she usually did. She put the key in the lock, let herself in and shut the door.

16

———

I LEFT WORK AN HOUR EARLY on Friday night. Mickey and I had wiped out every order on the board. Usually if we finished early we swept the floor, oiled tools or weeded flyers off the bulletin board but that Friday we snuck out the back door and hoped Enrique didn't notice. I suggested food logs for supper but Mickey had a date with Sheila, so I went home.

I had spoken on the phone to Whitney both evenings since the Tuesday night BONG meeting. Wednesday night she was chipper bordering on manic and told me stories about her clients. My revelation of the night before, as well as her reaction, sat in my stomach like a boulder, but she didn't mention it so neither did I. On Thursday night she was different, quiet and distracted. She would not tell me what was wrong, then started to cry. Neither of us suggested, either evening, that we spend the night together.

On Friday afternoon as I came down the walkway to my cottage I looked forward to our biking date the next day. We planned to ride the Pinehurst loop and I hoped to seduce her along the way, make love in the brush beside the road, something like that. I needed the feel of earth against my body. I wanted the reassurance of her skin, her hands, the exact size of her body against mine.

It was another one of those hot summer evenings, the air ripe with the smells of fruit trees and the bay. A beer and barbecued chicken night, I decided. Halfway down the walk I turned around to go back out for the groceries but stopped when I heard the sound of hard shoes crunching on gravel. I walked back to my cottage. Whitney, dressed in peach pumps and a peach business suit with a cream blouse, was fumbling at my door. My first thought was how badly she looked in that color. She looked washed out, like one big swath of pale paint. When she saw me her face reddened, becoming the brightest spot in the whole ensemble. I wondered what she was doing in a business suit and what she was doing here at a time I usually was at work. I forced a smile, made myself expect a special gift, a surprise.

I remember the next couple of moments in slow motion. I moved forward, my hands clean but still grease-stained, reaching for her. I saw the piece of paper she just had tucked between the doorjamb and doorknob. She drew back, I thought because of my greasy hands and her peach suit. I said, "I've washed them. It's just stain." That was when the look on her face registered. "What's wrong?" I asked, stopping my approach, feeling my center freeze and the iciness spread outward.

"It won't work, Lori," she said in a voice lower than her usual one.

"What won't?"

She stared straight at me, then waved at the patch of yard, my cottage, as if to indicate not just me but my entire environment, anything associated with me. She said, "Us."

Coolly I asked, "Is that what the note says?"

She nodded.

I picked up a rotten lemon, covered with a crust of white mold, and hurled it over the fence. I thought I screamed, "I can't read your frickin' note!" but a moment after the words came from my mouth I realized I only had whispered.

Whitney was silent for a long time, then she said, "You said you could read some. Was that a lie too?"

"What's your note say?" I asked in another scream-whisper.

She took the piece of paper and handed it to me. I refused to take it. "No," I said, "read it to me."

"It just says—"

"I said *read* it!" Finally a real shout.

I scared her. She opened the folded paper and looked at her note. Her hands shook so much the paper rustled. Suddenly she wadded it up and threw it at the lemon tree. "Fuck you, Lori. Read it yourself."

"You don't get it, do you? What I told you on Tuesday night."

But she got it. She got it all too well.

"What, Daddy wouldn't like it if you were dating someone who never went to college? Is that it?"

"It has nothing to do with your ... your illiteracy."

I felt the word like a slap.

She said, "This is about lying. This is about trust." Her ears were so red they looked like they were about to ignite. "If you'd told me right away—"

"If I'd told you right away," I interrupted, "you would have politely stopped returning my calls."

"Oh what bullshit. Don't feel so sorry for yourself. Everything about you is smoke and mirrors. You even made up the bike shop, didn't you? There's never going to be a bike shop, is there? That was all a game, something you thought would impress me."

"Maybe you should think about how much it did impress you. Maybe the idea of a booming business interested you a lot more than I did. Think about that."

Whitney did her imitation of a sea anemone, everything folded in. She said, "I'm sorry. There's no trust left in this relationship." She tried to step around me. I grabbed her arm. "Let go of me."

I held on long enough to say, "Is this real? You're leaving now?"

"I've had two sessions with my therapist since you told me Tuesday night. She says we're an inappropriate match."

I let go of her arm. "So I'm breaking up with your therapist. What do *you* think Whitney? Or do you?"

"I don't trust you anymore."

She pushed past me and as I listened to the clumsy clop of her pumps fade down the walkway to the street, the significance of the peach business suit hit me. The job with the graphics firm. I knew she'd taken it.

I entered my cottage and went to the bathroom where I found her greeting cards propped up on the window sill. Holding them like I held my flash cards, I laid down in the empty bathtub and traced the women's hips, breasts, mouths with my finger. *I hate seeing you give up on your dream*, she had told me not too long ago. Smoke and mirrors. I thought how she'd always seemed like a shell to me and realized I'd been listening for the roar ever since I met her. In those few stunned moments, immediately following her leaving me, I felt more tenderness toward Whitney than I ever had.

I tried calling her all weekend. Not only would she not answer the phone, she had turned off her answering machine so that I couldn't even leave a message. The woman had resolve, that was for sure. There was no question in my mind that it was over and the total absence of hope helped me in a way, helped me to leap right past the grieving phase. Maybe I would come back to it later, the sadness, but by Sunday night all I knew was that she was gone, *why* she was gone and that I was stone mad.

Monday morning I awoke to the realization that my only recourse if I was to communicate with her was to write.

I left three notes in her apartment building mail slot, one before work, one on my lunch hour and another after work, all written in fat, clumsy lettering without regard for spelling. I told her she had used me. I told her she didn't know smart when she saw it. I told her that with four years of college you would think she could figure out a lot more about life than she had. I told her she was the biggest coward. Did she really think leaving a note was an "appropriate" way to end a six-month relationship? To be mean I told her that her dad was right: She didn't have the guts to make it as an artist. I told her it would all come back to haunt her. I told her she looked dog-ugly in that peach suit.

On Tuesday I called in sick. I walked from Acton Street to Deirdre Felix's house up on Skyline, some ten miles. I sat hidden across the street in the bushes that used to have red berries and watched. Watched and thought. Nothing happened. No one came or went. What did I expect? Deirdre Felix to swoop out of her house in a Superwoman cape, snatch me up in her talons, fly me to another life?

In a way, yes. In a way, that was what she had begun to do, fly me to another life. Even in that moment as I nestled in the pulpy brown leaves and soil beneath the berry-less bushes, even as I raged at Whitney for robbing me of a certain small happiness, I took strength from looking at Deirdre Felix's house, knowing that inside was her study and all those books, realizing that even now I could feel her presence in my backbone.

I walked back down Tunnel Road, limping by the time I arrived at Whitney's doorstep moments before she came home from somewhere. I was sitting on the stairs when she arrived. She wore loose khaki chinos and a white cotton button down shirt, no business suit today, and a spasm of desire rippled through me. I stood up.

"I don't want to see you," she said, stepping by me and holding her key in front of her like a knife.

I placed my body between her and the keyhole.

"I'll call the police," she threatened and something inside me broke, broke hard.

I moved away from her door and stood on the stairs looking out on the street. I realized I hadn't spoken a word to her as I listened to the key enter the keyhole, the dead bolt slide out and the door open with a *whump* sound as the air got pushed aside. She slammed it shut.

The police? She had gone from "can't read" to "criminal" all in a few days, like the two were linked, like I was suspect now, possibly dangerous.

I hobbled home on feet that felt like stumps. I must have walked twenty miles that day. I climbed into bed and listened to my tape player all night, from the very beginning of my audio journal. Some time in the early morning, like three or two o'clock, I heard:

"Hi sweetie."

"Sweetie?"

"Oh loosen up. I can call you 'sweetie' if I want."

"I guess you can but I don't know if you can leave this here."

"I forgot it. An accident, okay?" A pause, then, "I have a surprise."

"What?"

"Where's an outlet?"

"What are you doing?"

"We're going to write the first draft of your business plan. It'll get you and Mickey going." Audible bustling. Then, "I can't believe you don't even have a table. Where do you eat? Where do you write? This will do. It'll be cozy. We can sit together on the bed and work.

"Lori, it'll be fun! We can get a draft out in two hours. Just wait, you'll feel so relieved to get it done."

"No."

"Lori—"

"No."

"I just thought—"

"We're having an affair. I didn't hire you to be my personal manager."

Then the *brrrr* sound of my phone ringing. I fast-forwarded past the part where I had talked to Deirdre Felix on the phone, past the part where Whitney had questioned me suspiciously and then I pressed "play." I heard giggling, rustling, moaning, thumping. Kind of like scrubbing the dirt out of a wound with a toothbrush, I replayed over and over again the part where Whitney came, loud and raw. Right afterwards, the tape had run out. The machine under the bed had clicked off. Whitney had perked up, asked, "What was that?" I had answered, "What was what?" and we had laughed, loved, talked some more.

17

My longing for Whitney's touch was sharp and ragged, a sawing in my chest. Not nearly so visceral but somehow bigger, taking up more space, was Deirdre Felix's absence from my life. My breakup with Whitney was like a car crash and Deirdre Felix's absence was the air bag that slammed into my face and chest. I thought I saw her everywhere. I would be in the grocery store and see her disappear around the canned foods aisle. I would go trotting over there only to find some other gray-haired, well-dressed woman. Then I would see her standing in line at a check-cashing store until I realized Deirdre Felix would never be at one of those stores. Sometimes I felt deserted by her. More often I felt regret for all my sarcasm, the times I had been sullen. Why hadn't I tried harder to tell her what she had given me? Of course there was the poem but that embarrassed rather than comforted me. I racked my brain trying to think of something real I could give her. But like what? What did Deirdre Felix need?

It was a hot dry July. I did not leave any more notes for

Whitney, I did not haunt Deirdre Felix's house again and I did not tell Mickey much about the breakup. I thought he might take Whitney's side, at least agreeing with the part about me being a liar. He still glowed with his devotion for Sheila and I got the feeling that my presence, my unhappy presence, tainted the purity of his bliss.

What I did do in those summer months was horde books. As if every book I held in front of me was a shield against Whitney's betrayal and simultaneously a magnet for Deirdre Felix's attention, I gathered books. I went to every branch of the Berkeley Public Library, except for Pam's branch, and checked them out. I checked out children's books, like Charles read. I checked out photography books and machine manuals. I checked out novels and magazines. A librarian in the downtown library showed me a section of gay and lesbian literature and I worked my way through those books. Which is not to say I *read* them. I checked them out. I let them pile up in my cottage, on my bed, on my kitchen counter, on the bathroom floor. And I held them. I had learned to love the cool crispness of the paper, the idea that the pages were like countries over which dozens of other pairs of eyes had traveled. I traveled too. Sometimes I did read, really read, sentences, figuring out words I didn't know or skipping them. Other times I just let my eyes roam over the black ink, the words, like they were part of a landscape. I had no idea where I was going but was determined to stay in that wilderness for as long as I could stand. Often that was only a minute or two. Occasionally it was a whole hour.

Other than my "reading" and going to work, I cycled hundreds of miles. Each evening after work I rode my mountain bike into the hills of the regional parks, grunting up steep dirt paths, bouncing down grassy slopes, racing the hawks, frightening rabbits. Each day off I climbed on the saddle of my handmade racer at dawn. Some mornings I rode out to Contra Costa County, miles into the country where there was nothing but cows and fields. Other mornings I rode across the Golden Gate Bridge and into Marin County, sucking in the startling ocean views, taking comfort in the thick tree trunks plush with moss. Cyclists call this kind of riding LSD, which stands for "long steady distance" but also means transformative riding, psychedelic riding, riding through your limits, beyond your limits, until your brain is bald of thought, your heart cleansed of fear and sorrow.

I collected books. I rode my bike. I waited for the next thing to happen.

At the beginning of August, three weeks after Whitney left and two months after Deirdre Felix quit, I climbed up on my landlady's rooftop at sunset. She was home so I shimmied up the drain pipe as quietly as I could. I reached my hand over the gutter, gripped the roofing shingles with my fingertips and hoped they held as I hefted the rest of myself up. I placed each bare foot softly, trying to creep noiselessly to the crest of the roof.

From there I could see in the last light of the day the hills to the east and the bay and bridges to the west. It was a simple sunset, nothing glorious or colorful, the bridges like skeletons against the rusty sky, the bay as flat and hard and cold as a sheet of steel.

I lay down, arching my back across the roof's crown, and looked at the sky made bright and perpetually starless by the city lights. I had no great revelations but a stillness opened inside me, a quiet.

And in that quiet came two funny thoughts. The first one was that Whitney, wanting to end our relationship after I told her I couldn't read, had tried to do so with a note. Tonight that made me smile. The second funny thought was that I had unleashed my anger at her with a series of notes, with writing. My fury had roared like a tsunami over my self-consciousness. My need to communicate with her had been greater than my shame. Even in that moment. Especially in that moment. I pictured my notes, each only a sentence or two long, words spelled any old way with big chunky letters. This struck me as very funny and I stood on the crest of the roof and did a little barefoot dance, pointing my toes and spinning like a cartoon ballerina. I pranced nimble-footed to the front of the house, then back to the other end, balancing on the crown of the roof like it was a tight rope. As I danced, the lights in the hills began to blink on. Still dancing, now a jig more than a ballet, I faced east, south, west, then north. I was considering adding a chant to my dance when, facing north, I saw the police car pull up in front of my landlady's house.

Two officers jumped out and busted in our gate. I crouched down, then flopped onto my belly, pressing myself as close to the roof as I could. I heard one say, "I'll take the back. You watch the front." Then my landlady's voice at the front door, followed by the cop shouting, "Stay inside, ma'am, stay inside!" My heart pounded against the roofing shingles.

As the light flashed back and forth across my body plastered to the roof I had a strong feeling of déjà vu. Then I remembered the sensored lights coming on as I snuck around in the woods outside Deirdre Felix's house. Despite the gravity of the present situation I had an overwhelming urge to laugh. That urge was snuffed out quickly when the bright light settled on me and stopped.

"Don't move," the cop ordered.

This was highly embarrassing. This really took the cake. I had done it now.

My voice was a squeak as I tried, "I live here."

I heard the other cop rush from the front of the house to back up his buddy on the patio. I could not see much looking into the glaring light but felt certain both had guns pointing at me. I said again, louder, "I *live* here."

"Very slowly, stand up." I did as I was told. "Move to the edge of the roof. Same place you got up there."

I walked carefully down the slope to the drainage pipe, concentrating on the feel of the roofing shingle grit against the soles of my feet. I stopped and waited for my next orders. "I live here," I said again but the cop told me to shut up. I could see them both now. One stood with his legs braced apart, the gun in both hands, pointed at me, just like they do on television. The other one was the talker.

"Come on down, kid," he said. "Same way you went up."

Shimmying up the drainage pipe had been hard enough and I had done it without an audience. Going down would be even more difficult. Yet it was too far to jump. Get real, I told myself, this is no time to indulge feelings of performance anxiety. I mean, what did I care how agile I looked getting off this roof? I licked my palms to make them sticky, then held onto the pipe and swung my legs over the edge of the roof. I braced my bare feet against the side of the house and clung to the pipe. My next move was not obvious. I felt paralyzed.

"Down," ordered the officer.

So I pretended the drainage pipe was a Maypole and I slid. The drainage pipe, however, was not a Maypole. It had bumps and knobs that on my way down tore at the insides of my thighs and arms. I crashed onto the pavement feeling bruised but not defeated. Against all reason my spirits were still dancing.

"It's a woman," the talking cop said. "Lady, what the hell were you doing?"

"I live here," I repeated. "I was looking at the view."

"Go get the lady up front," the officer in charge told his crony.

"I'm sorry," I said the moment she came out the back door onto the patio. "I didn't think you were home," I lied.

"Lori," she said. "My god, it's you."

I nodded, tried for a smile, managed a grimace.

"You know her?"

"Yes of course. She's my tenant."

"Jesus," the cop mumbled lowering his gun. He demanded, "What were you doing on the roof?"

"Looking at the view," I repeated.

He looked at my landlady. She waved him away. "It's okay," she said. "You can go."

Both officers shook their heads, tossed me looks of contempt and left.

My landlady looked tired and embarrassed.

"I'm really sorry," I told her.

"Don't you ever again," was all she said before going back in the patio door and locking it.

At work the next day I told Mickey, "I'm developing a disturbing behavior pattern."

"What's that?"

I told him in full detail about spying on Deirdre Felix's husband and the blue-clad bimbo, followed by the whole story of what had happened the night before. Though at first Mickey looked alarmed, by the end of my stories he was laughing. Loudly. Enrique came from the front of the shop and said the entire store could hear us. We apologized, then after Enrique left, planned my new career as a burglar, targeting Arnie's office for my first break-in. It was fun, like old times, clowning with Mickey.

That afternoon, probably as punishment for being rowdy, Enrique told me and Mickey we had to clear the board before leaving for the night. At five o'clock there were only two repairs left and I didn't have anything to do after work so I told Mickey to go ahead home. It had been a long time since I was in the shop alone, something I used to love.

After finishing the repairs, I walked out into the retail part of the store. I still had that quiet in me from the rooftop, in spite of the interruption by the police, in spite of my clowning with Mickey. And now standing alone in the dark bike shop surrounded by cranks, tires, freewheels, derailleurs, headsets, I felt in them the presence of great possibility. I started to trip on the gorgeousness of wheels, the way the spokes spray out from the hub like some futuristic flower, and on the perfect economy of a tight gear cluster, each tooth anticipating the grace of a well-oiled chain. I started to think that maybe I would build a new bike this fall, from scratch, when my eyes found the green hybrid.

It had been there for a few weeks, on sale because it was last year's model. I would get my employee's discount on top of that. A tasteful deep green, the color of the plants she so loved, with black trim. Not a trace of day-glo, which I was sure would repel her. I would never buy myself a hybrid—not really a mountain bike, not really a touring bike and definitely not a racing bike—but people gravitated toward them because they looked easy. They looked possible. I knew Deirdre Felix needed easy and possible.

I took the bike with me that night. I considered writing a note like the ones I had written Whitney in my beginner's scrawl, saying I would pay for the bicycle tomorrow—the idea gave me that buoyant feeling again, like I was filled with a frothy intelligence all my own—but I was not quite ready for my coworkers to inspect my writing skills. I would just call Enrique tonight so he wouldn't freak when he found the bicycle missing tomorrow.

I walked home pushing my own bike in one hand and the new bike in the other. A breeze off the bay freshened the city-hot air. I looked at the green bike and smiled at its silly gawkiness compared to the graceful lines of my racer. Kind of a reversal of me and Deirdre Felix.

It was close to seven-thirty by the time I got to Acton Street. I called Enrique and told him I had the bike and intended to pay for it. He lopped off another ten percent and I said, "For a pain-in-the-butt boss, you're all right." I made him so uncomfortable with my little admission of affection, he forgot to say goodbye before hanging up. Good old Enrique.

I grabbed a helmet and the tools I would need to fit the bike to Deirdre Felix, lifted it onto my car's bike rack and drove up to Skyline Boulevard. I arrived at dusk.

A man who looked a little like Clint Eastwood, rugged with beard stubble and pinched, graying good looks was climbing into the BMW parked in the driveway, not the garage, as if poised for a getaway. I knew it was Arnie. Just by his looks, Hollywood superficial, I could tell that even if he did love music, he did not love the ballet. There was nothing subtle in the language of his body.

His movements getting in the car were springy, like he thought having sex with a younger woman made him someone. I tried to imagine how he would look and move if he'd had a life performing music instead of surgery. Would the path have been similar, just a variation of the one he was on, or radically different, unimaginable to the man he now was? I wondered if a part of him still loved Deirdre Felix. I flashed back on the second time I met Deirdre Felix, that day in the library when she told me I reminded her of Arnie. She had said, "I've lived with a hustler for thirty-nine years. I know all the signs." I wondered if a ventriloquist and a hustler were similar.

I waited in the street until he backed out of the driveway, then pulled into the spot where the BMW had been parked. I carried the helmet and pushed the bike up to the front door, moving so fast the plants stirred as I passed. I rang the bell. I had not forgotten the poem but decided to act as if I had.

Classical music blasted from the open upstairs windows. Maybe she couldn't hear me. I was about to ring the doorbell again when I heard someone drag the needle across the record, surely destroying it. Then I heard several sharp cracks as if someone were breaking the record into pieces.

Good judgment told me to go home and come back another time. Instead I rang the bell again.

I about died when Deirdre Felix yanked open the door because I could tell she thought I was Arnie returning. Her face was wild with accusation and her gray hair, usually fluffy and neat, fell limply from the crown of her head. She wore an unironed cotton blouse marked with a pale coffee stain. In her raised fist she held a bunch of sharp triangular vinyl pieces, like black taco chips. I flinched because it looked as if she were about to throw them in my face.

We both stared until she said, "Lori. This is a very bad time."

I wanted to run yet felt the dusk behind me thickening into something permanent and impenetrable, making the only possible movement forward. I said, "You look awful. Was that Arnie?"

I motioned behind me with a cocked thumb.

I had never seen anger inhabit a body so entirely as it did hers. She jerked with aggravation, like she was restraining herself from kicking or mauling me. "I'll have to ask you to—"

"I'm leaving. Right now. But this bike is staying with you. Someone left it at the shop and never picked it up." That was a lie of course. I would pay cash for the bike the next day but I knew she would never accept it as a gift. "I know you think you don't want it. I also know that you might feel better if you ride it. I'll show you how. Later, I mean."

"No thank you. Goodbye."

I had not seen Deirdre Felix in two months. Yet in a strange, phantom kind of way she had been my main companion. This was not the reunion I wanted. I put my foot in the door. "Are you okay? You look awful."

"You said that already." She looked at my sneaker.

"I promise you'll feel better if you bring this bike and meet me Saturday morning—"

"What makes you think you know anything about what would make me feel better?"

Her words scorched but I took them to be a real question, like I was supposed to answer. "I know I'm young. I've never been married. I've never even been in a relationship for longer than a couple of years." I paused. She was actually listening. "But I know riding this bike will make you feel better. I do know that. Biking is movement, movement created by you the cyclist, real movement through real space. When you ride a bike, you feel as if you're pulling the landscape through your lungs." I was amazed at what came out of my mouth. "Meet me at eight o'clock Saturday morning at the Breezeway Market. Down by the Berkeley Marina. I'll show you how to ride."

"Take your foot out of the door."

When I didn't, I saw the muscles in her neck and shoulders loosen a tiny bit. I straightened my own shoulders and raised my chin.

"Please, Lori."

"You could listen to me. You might learn something."

She almost smiled.

I removed my foot.

She stared for a moment at the place it had been. "Come in," she said. "For one second."

I laughed out of awkwardness. After propping the bike against the house, I followed her into the front room. I had walked by this room many times on my way to the study but never actually entered it.

She slumped onto the couch. I sat down carefully on the other end of it. Dusk occupied the room entirely and she made no move to turn on lights. A faint bad smell, like spoiled food or the presence of a sick person, tinged the air. A big photo of a young man sat on the mantle. Jeff, the architect son, I supposed. Why wasn't he coming down from Seattle to straighten out his asshole father?

For once silence did not make me uneasy. I waited.

Finally she smiled and for a moment she was the old gracious Deirdre Felix. "You caught me at a very bad moment. Yes that was Arnie." *Pfft*, went her mouth. Then, "A bike, huh? When I was a girl I loved biking. That's lovely, what you just said, about the landscape."

I nodded encouragement.

"This whole thing with Arnie and the younger woman . . . what a cliché." She stood up. "Fuck them both."

I laughed, said, "That's the spirit."

"Thank you for the bike. Maybe I'll try it." She waited, still standing. So I stood and she walked me to the door.

"Riding a bike is easy," I said, thrilled that she was keeping it, then pushed my luck. "But there's a lot of technique too. I'll give you a lesson on Saturday morning."

"Oh I don't know." She opened the door and looked out past the green bicycle into the garden, distracted.

"Think about it," I pressed. I wanted my gift to be much more than a machine. "I'll be riding Saturday morning either way. I

158

usually get coffee at the Breezeway Market around eight"—yet another lie, but harmless—"so meet me if you want."

"Goodbye, Lori." I did not like the firmness in her voice.

"Not all hustlers are bad, you know," I told her. "Some hustlers push for the good of others, not just themselves."

"Goodbye, Lori." Not even a hint of a smile.

I hesitated a moment longer. Annoyance flooded her eyes. I left.

18

―――――――

"Oh, Mick I'm so sorry," I said for about the tenth time. How could I have been so flippant about what a kiss meant? Or what sex meant. Smack, you do it. What was I thinking?

Sitting across from him in the Vietnamese restaurant in downtown Oakland, all I wanted was to protect him from this pain. At least his hair had grown out completely by now, and the way he wore it tied back in a ponytail, the strands no longer flopping in his face, made him look tougher, sort of alternative, maybe like a rock musician, or even possibly, with a long stretch of the imagination, like some burly biker's—as in Hell's Angel's—sidekick.

In my dreams.

The fact was, I could not stop thinking of his slender chest engraved with the long, brown scar that on another man, on a man with skin less like mocha satin, would be a badge of masculinity. On Mickey, the one time I had glimpsed his naked chest, the scar made him look threadbare, like it could burst apart at any moment. I wondered what sex would be like with a man like

Mickey who was not jaded about his body, or about a woman's body. I imagined Sheila touching that scar and grew angry thinking that she probably didn't have any idea what she had had in Mickey.

Mickey's eyes were red-rimmed and his long black lashes crusty. He had ordered beef tendon soup and twisted the noodles around on his chopsticks without eating. I felt responsible, like I had pushed him out of an airplane with a parachute and forgot to tell him that sometimes the thing didn't open. Sometimes you fell on your face. A kiss, smack, what's the big deal? Stupid me.

The good news, according to Mickey, was that Sheila had not rejected him. He said that she said that she still loved him. What happened, according to Sheila, was that her father found out. He insisted she stop seeing Mickey. He threatened to kick her out of the house, she said, he threatened to withdraw funding for college.

"What do you think," Mickey asked, "is it because I'm ten years older than her, because I'm Latino or because I look like I do?"

"What do I think, what?" I asked, stalling.

"Her parents," he said. "Why they won't let her see me."

"No one likes a guy having sex with their daughter," I said, knowing that it was the ten years, his being Latino, the way he looked, all three.

"Yeah," he said. "Okay, yeah."

I was pretty nervous about the father part. Sheila was under-age, after all. There was a legal word for Mickey's relationship with her, a felony word.

"Mick," I asked gently, "did Sheila say anything about her father, you know, like coming after you?"

"I don't know," Mickey mumbled as if that were the least of his worries. He twisted more noodles with his chopsticks, stared blindly into the meat soup.

"Does he know where you live?"

Mickey shrugged.

Should I be driving him to the Mexican border? Sure it was fucked up for an older man to seduce a legal child, if that was what had happened, but real life complicated good theory. It was hard for me to think of Sheila as the victim in this situation, at least not the only victim.

"Mickey." I took his hand. "How did her father find out?"

"Sheila's very honest. She hated the sneaking around part."

"That means she *told* him?"

Mickey nodded, looking miserably proud of her honesty. Sheila the goddess of all virtues. When I was in tenth grade and in love for the first time, I too believed my beloved was perfect, as in one hundred percent flawless, but Mickey was twenty-seven years old. I guessed it was a first-time kind of thing, no matter how old you were, probably all the more excruciating for his having waited for so long.

I wasn't getting anywhere pursuing this father thing, so I tried another tack. "What do you think Sheila will do?"

"Do?" he moaned.

"Yeah, I mean, will she accept her parents' not letting her see you?"

He sat up straighter in the booth and looked at me hard. "She's only sixteen. She either puts up with it or runs away. And that's not an option. Not for her, anyway. She's going to college and everything."

"Would it be an option for *you?*" As sweltering as it was in the restaurant, I shivered at the idea of Mickey being on the run with a sixteen-year-old girl.

"I told her we could get married," he said glumly.

"Mickey!" I yelled. "You can't do that!"

He looked at me like I would never understand, like I had never been in love. He had big dark circles under his eyes and his whole face looked like it was going to collapse to one side.

"Don't worry," he said. "She wouldn't marry me. I told you. She has big ambitions. College and stuff."

Mickey slammed his chopsticks down on the table and clenched his jaw. He looked out the window onto Oakland's Franklin Street. For a moment the sweet naiveté in his eyes hardened into something more common in a man his age, a flat wariness.

That was when it hit me and I knew he knew it too. Sheila lied. Her parents never found out anything. They didn't know he was ten years older, they didn't know he was Latino, they didn't know what his face looked like. Sheila's parents didn't know Mickey existed. She dumped him, pure and simple.

Oh, Mickey.

He picked up his chopsticks and lifted a piece of tendon out of his bowl.

"Put that down," I said, swallowing a gag.

Mickey dropped the nasty animal innard and asked, "What do I do now?"

"What do you mean?"

"The whole world is different, jagged and lethal, out of focus and blunt, all at once. How can I just go to work, come home, watch TV? What happens next?"

I suppressed a smile. Okay, Mickey was no Hell's Angel, never would be, but there was something new in his chest, a fist of anger and pain behind that scar. And in Mickey, I welcomed it. Not the pain of course, but the gristle it would bring, the knowledge.

I leaned back in the booth and fingered the duct tape that failed to close a long tear in the vinyl. I did have an answer to Mickey's question: What happens next? The constant sawing in my chest had changed into a bruise that hurt only if I touched it. And just recently I started to feel love again, plain old generic unassigned love, trickling through my veins like blood. But I knew better than to offer an answer now. He was way too raw. In a few weeks maybe. Still, just knowing there was an answer made me happy. I accidentally laughed.

Mickey said, "What's so damn funny?"

"I got you back. That makes me happy."

Mickey pulled my hand across the table and held it against his zipper lips. "At least I got you," he said as his eyes filled with tears.

"You got me," I whispered. I took my hand away from his lips and reached between the buttons of his shirt, touching the place where the scar would be. "You definitely got me."

Saturday morning was foggy and cold as I rode down to the marina. In another hour or two, folks would be out doing errands but for the moment it was quiet and still, as if the thick fog held everything stationary. Everything but me. I sliced through the wet, gray air on my custom-built bicycle, worrying about Mickey. He wasn't sleeping or eating, and I had to call him the last two mornings and talk him into coming to work.

My own appetite, however, was quite healthy. When I got to the Breezeway Market I zeroed in on the espresso stand. I ordered two croissants and a mocha, then stood straddling my bike as I ate and drank.

"You're late."

Her voice shot like an arrow through the insulating fog and penetrated my groggy head, startling me so much I dropped the mocha. Before I did anything else, I retrieved it and thanks to the lid did not lose much.

Of course I had come down here to meet Deirdre Felix, but I had not expected her to show up, not even a little bit. She sat on the bench a few yards from the coffee vendor and apparently had been there as I rode up and ordered my croissants and mocha.

"Sorry," she said. "I thought you saw me."

I shook my head.

She said, "I'm not a morning person myself. I figured you didn't speak because you needed your coffee first."

I maneuvered a smile onto my face. Between the scare, the fact that I *did* need coffee and my amazement that she had shown up, I was speechless.

Deirdre Felix wore a shiny pink, lavender and white warm-up suit. She already had a black grease smudge on the inside of her right pant leg. She stood. "Finish your coffee," she said.

"It's mocha," I corrected. My heart pounded much harder than the situation called for. So she showed up. So she was riding the deep green bicycle with black trim. I guess I was awed that I actually influenced Deirdre Felix, I actually caused her to do something.

She looked out of place, awkwardly grasping the bicycle's handlebars, as out of place as she had looked that day at the bus stop. Deirdre Felix in the early morning at the Berkeley marina holding a green bicycle? Yet she had come. Which meant that maybe I really had figured out something she needed.

I eyeballed the height of the top tube compared to the length of her legs. The bike fit well enough for now.

"Come on." My voice came out gruff and commanding, though my heart still ricocheted off my rib cage. I stuffed down the remaining bite of my second croissant and tossed the half-finished mocha toward the trash barrel five feet away, suffering a moment of panic before it fell expertly in the center of the can. I waved Deirdre Felix onto the road. "Follow me."

I set off down Frontage Road, looking back every couple of seconds. She was more wobbly on the bike than seemed safe, so I dropped back to ride behind her where I could keep a look out. The change startled her and she lost balance. As the bike teetered, she kicked out her legs for equilibrium and managed not to fall over.

"You're in too high a gear," I told her. "Shift down at least two."

I cringed listening to the grinding of her gears as she tried to get the chain seated in the sprockets. "This gear is too easy," she yelled back to me after she finally got it. "My legs aren't doing any work."

"That's where I want you to be. Just spin the pedals easily."

"My feet fly off in this low gear!"

"Concentrate on pedaling in a full circle."

"Why this low gear?"

I enjoyed her exasperation. "I want you to get the feel of correct pedaling technique before anything else," I yelled forward. "It's about discipline to detail."

Deirdre Felix did not look behind her so she didn't see my huge grin. She did quiet down about the low gear though.

We rode on silently for a few minutes, me mindful of not giving her too much instruction all at once. I ignored the already heavy freeway traffic just beyond the thick shrubbery to our left and looked out at the bay beginning about ten feet off my right pedal. High tide. The August heat of the past weeks had drawn the stink from the bay, the air was saturated with it, but at this early hour, and with the fog, it was a smell of *fresh* garbage, almost like a beauty mark, tingeing the riches of water and air. It occurred to me that before pollution, people probably didn't even know what fresh was.

A homeless family—a man, woman and two children—sat on the shore rocks tossing bits of bread, their breakfast, to sea gulls. Deirdre Felix must have looked at them too and lost her concentration, because that was when she went down.

"I'm fine. I'm fine. I'm fine," was all she said as she got up, brushed off her shiny warm-up suit, now shredded on the outside of the left thigh, and remounted her bike. Her mouth was set hard and she looked almost mean as she said, "I'm ready. Let's go."

"Are you sure you're okay?"

"Let's go."

"You're very butch," I said.

"Butch?" she asked. "What do you mean?"

I relished knowing a word, at least a specific meaning of a word, that Deirdre Felix did not know. I demonstrated by remaining silent, climbing on my bike and taking off again.

When we reached the Emeryville marina, we turned around and rode back to Berkeley. Deirdre Felix wasn't a half-bad cyclist for a beginner, though she almost fell off the bike again, this time at a stop sign, and crunched the gears a lot. She didn't hurt herself though and I could tune up the bike later.

By the time we got back to the Breezeway Market, we had ridden a total of five miles and the sun was just finishing off the fog. I watched Deirdre Felix dismount. Her limbs looked shaky but

166

there was a film of sweat on her face and a bit of spitfire in her eyes.

"You ruined your warm-up suit," I told her, motioning to the blackened leg and torn fabric.

"*Pfft*," she said. "It was a stupid thing to wear biking."

"I'm glad you showed up."

"I wasn't going to," she said, then realized her rudeness. "I mean, I just didn't see how . . . well, anyway. I had to do something to get out of the house. Last night I ran into Arnie at a restaurant. He was with Tina."

"Wow," I said. What a name, Tina.

"I made a scene." She coughed out a severe laugh. "I don't believe I've ever made a scene in public before. I was with my mother who's eighty-five years old." She dropped her face in her hands and moaned, "Oh god." The bike, which I guess she forgot she was holding, crashed onto the gravel. There went the beautiful green paint job. "Oh!" she said and left it there. "We were waiting for a table. It was bad enough that Mother had to see me smoking. When I saw them sitting across the dining room, I went right over and put my cigarette out on Tina's grilled mahi mahi."

"Wow," I said again, impressed.

Our eyes met and Deirdre Felix burst out laughing.

"I can't believe I'm laughing," she howled. She wiped her eyes, tried to stop, then gave in to it. "Then . . . then . . . I took Arnie's glass of red wine and threw it on her white silk blouse. Right on her size D silicon tits."

She bent over and put her hands on her knees, panting with laughter. I thought maybe I should try to stabilize her, guide her to the bench or something, but she stood up and with tears streaming down her face, tried to go on between sobs of emotion, "The thing is . . . the thing is, Arnie doesn't even know I'm smoking again!" For some reason this was hysterically funny to her. "And my mother doesn't even know Arnie and I are getting divorced!"

She finally calmed down, looked me in the eye and chuckled

a little more. I had a brief retaliation fantasy of me, decked in ultra-dyke gear, taking Deirdre Felix to dinner in some fancy restaurant and having Arnie walk in. I liked to think it would drive him wild to see his wife with a woman like me though of course he would probably just laugh.

"You okay?" I asked.

"Of course I'm not okay. But Lori, this bike ride was wonderful. Just getting out of my head. Exercise and those marvelous endorphins."

I pointed to the top of Grizzly Peak in the distance. "One day we're going to get you up there."

"I live up there."

"I know that. I mean ride from here."

"On my bike? I don't think so."

"It's not that hard. Wait and see."

She narrowed her eyes and looked up at Grizzly Peak. "*Pfft,*" she dismissed it.

"Next Saturday," I said. "Same place, same time."

I expected her to withdraw again but she shook out each leg and said, "We'll see. This really was lovely. Thank you."

The following Saturday I arrived good and early. I was sitting on the bench sipping my mocha when Deirdre Felix drove up in a rental car. I waited for her to unload her bike from the trunk, then watched her ride across the gravel parking lot. She braked in front of me, smiling, her crumply cheeks poofing out around the straps of her helmet. I glanced up at Grizzly Peak. The day was already hot and clear; little waves of heat shimmered over the highest point in the East Bay hills.

"I practiced every day this week," she told me.

"You're a better student than I am," I answered gruffly to cover up my pleasure.

"Just desperate."

I laughed. I didn't care if I was her answer to desperate. After all, she'd been mine.

I corrected her form, raised the saddle an inch and tried to teach her about gear ratios. She wasn't ready for that, so I sighed heavily and tried to sound annoyed as I said, "We'll just ride."

Out of the corner of my eye I saw her smile.

An hour later, when we got back to the Breezeway Market, she said, "I never thanked you for the poem."

My stomach flipped and I broke out in a fresh sweat. I'd convinced myself that she hadn't gotten the poem after all, that for once the post office had fucked up at an opportune time, or that I'd written the address incorrectly.

In her stern tutor's voice, she said, "It's very good. Lovely."

My head got hot and giddy. That strict voice of approval hit much deeper than any mushy praise could have.

"However," she went on, "'elegant' is misspelled. It's e-l-e-g-*a*-n-t."

I could have killed Mickey.

Then she said, "Thank you, Lori. You're wonderful."

19

Pam had gained weight and permed her now shoulder-length hair. It fluffed and curled around her bright cheeks like doll's hair. Well, maybe a feral doll. No matter how hard she tried for respectability Pam would always look untamed which was what made me want to touch her, even after all this time. She still had those sideways black exclamation mark eyebrows and she still wore oversized earrings, stirrup pants and a big sweater. Today's sweater was multi-colored squares and the pants were bright blue, definitely an outfit designed to please children. I set the bicycle book on the counter in front of her and said, "Hi."

"Well hi."

"I'm sorry about running out with this book a few months ago." I had not planned any confessions, but heard myself saying, "Libraries are difficult places for me. I'm a new reader. I used to be with the literacy program. But I think you already know that."

"Really?" She smiled too hard. "You don't look like, I mean, you don't seem like. . . ." She waved her hand in embarrassment.

"Yeah, well. I just wanted to apologize for acting so funny that day. And for sort of stealing this book. It was an accident."

Her stressed face softened. "I already cleared your card on the computer. There are no fines or anything."

"Thanks. Here. I brought you something else." I put the small package on the counter next to the bicycle repair book. I had even bought pastel yellow wrapping paper. She picked up the gift and the toy inside rattled. "It's for the baby."

"Lori, that's so sweet!" I could tell she was genuinely touched by the gift and I was genuinely touched she remembered my name.

"Boy or girl?"

"Boy. His name is Grant."

"He's gotta be, what, a year old now?"

"Five and a half months."

"Oh right. I'm bad at babies. Anyway, I was wondering if you could recommend a book. Like an easy one with a good story."

A few minutes later I left the library with a book called *Desert of the Heart*, same story as the movie *Desert Hearts*. Pam wasn't sure how easy the book was but I told her not to worry. I liked checking it out and I liked the heft of it in my hands, whether I could read it or not.

Once out the library door, I stopped and looked at the cinder block building. Slow motion set in again. From this moment right on through the next hour. I floated back to the door, grasped the handle, pulled it open. I told Pam, who was still at the check-out desk, that I thought I would read for a while. I walked to the back of the library and instead of taking a seat at a table, stood in the open Literacy Project door. They were all there, the participants in the new readers writing class, with a teacher standing up front.

This wasn't a coincidence of course. I'd gotten the flyer a few weeks ago, written in simple words and printed in big letters, followed up by a call from Marilyn. I never planned to come but the date of the first class, August twentieth, got stamped on my brain. Some other part of my brain got that clever idea about making amends with Pam and put the whole gig together. Then of course there was the part about wanting to get Deirdre Felix to the top of Grizzly Peak on her bike. Sometimes I make deals with myself. For one thing to happen, I have to do another thing. Balance. Karmic debt. No such thing as a free lunch. Call it what you want, but here I was at the Literacy Project's writing class.

As I stood in the doorway unable to leave and unable to enter, I felt as if there were a whole corporation in my head, run by millions of brain cell committees, all making contradictory decisions.

The next moment, when everybody in the class noticed me, was a lot like the first time I ever went to a lesbian bar, only much worse. When I came out about ten years ago, I took a field trip to Amelia's in San Francisco. All I saw as I stepped into the bar were very short haircuts and thick leather jackets. I nearly blacked out. The difference between that evening and this one was that as much as those women scared me, I harbored a secret and intense admiration for them. As I entered the bar, as they turned and stared at the newcomer, a seed of possibility thrilled to life inside me.

I did not harbor similar feelings for these new readers. Only the fear.

The teacher, who was mid-sentence, stopped talking and turned to look at me along with the rest of the class, a dozen full-grown people who could neither read nor write. As plain as day, as if they were real, I heard voices, the jeering of schoolchildren, voices I'd heard for years in elementary school. *Mental case. Retard. MR. Dummy.*

I heard my father's voice too, scratchy and comforting. *My girl's smarter than any of 'em. Lori's too bright for that school.*

I saw Mrs. Roach's bright red thin lips, wispy ponytail, last chance eyes.

If I stepped into this room what would it mean? One on one with Deirdre Felix was one thing. A group, community, joining, belonging, that was another.

My hand let go of the door and I took a step back just as Charles stood and said, "Hey, good to see you. Lori, right? There's a seat right here." He scooted a chair in next to him and made space for me. I entered the room and walked, still in slow motion, over to the chair and sat down.

"Sorry I'm late," I mumbled.

The teacher said, "We were just getting ready to write."

She told the rest of the class, "Go ahead and begin."

Then she came over and explained what she had already explained to the others. Writing, she said quietly, was a lot like cooking or playing a sport. Did you learn cooking by reading cookbooks? Did you learn a sport by studying rule books? No, of course not. You learned by doing, stumbling through your mistakes, practicing. She told me to write about a person who meant a lot to me. For now I was to forget about spelling and grammar. We would deal with that later. She said to just get my thoughts down on the paper. If I wanted her or one of the tutors in the room to write the words for me, I could dictate. Did I want to think for a moment? I nodded. She left to help another learner, promising to return. I noticed a couple of people who looked like tutors hovering on the edges of the room. A couple other tutors sat next to learners, carefully writing down their spoken words, just as Deirdre Felix had done for me.

I took a deep breath of the air, feeling as if I had to suck at it hard to get any oxygen. I picked up the pencil to ward off the tutors. My hands were clammy. I put the point of the pencil on the piece of notebook paper sitting on the table in front of me and with my head bent down, looked around the room.

The tables were set up in a horseshoe. Lillian sat across from me, wearing a blue floral print house dress, and was already scribbling away on her pad of paper, smiling to herself. Moving only my eyes, not my head, I glanced at Charles's paper. He had written in big block letters, "My wif Sheryl."

I did not want the teacher to come back so I figured I had better write something. I wrote, "My frind Witney." The teacher circled back anyway.

"How's it going, Lori?"

"Fine."

I held the pencil hard, breaking the tip on the paper, and waited for her to get away from me.

She had straight blond hair and a thin pointed nose. Her skin was so pale her temples were blue. Something about her reminded me of Mrs. Roach. "I'm fine," I said again and she wandered off.

I erased what I had written, then wrote it again. As a defense against the roaming teacher and tutors, I decided to put my pencil on the paper and keep writing as long as I could, no matter what. "My frind Whitney. Shes an ardis. She likes the truth. Her hart wants to be open. But shes afrad other peopels failyer is contajus. Wat she thinks is other peopels failyer. I lid to her. We are no longer frinds."

I read my piece silently and felt a flash of pride. It was the longest thing I'd ever written on my own. Then I felt hot all over again. I heard the children jeering. I put my open-faced hand on top of the paper and began to squeeze my fingers together, gathering the sheet into a wad, but Charles grabbed my fist. I was so startled I jumped and made a funny little sound. He laughed.

"Wait," he said. "Don't throw it away." Then he put his paper on top of mine. "Look at this," he said. "What do you think?"

I looked on as he read his story to me. "My wif Sheryl. Sheryl is the most beeyutiful woman I no. She is good muther. We met in 1978. We bin together for 18 yer."

"Eighteen years," I said. "How'd you do that?"

He shrugged, smiled.

"I never managed longer than two years with anyone."

"Takes work," Charles said. "A lot of work. Who did you write about?"

I looked at my paper. "Friend of mine. We had a falling out."

"Mmm. Sorry to hear that."

The teacher stood in front of the class again and asked who wanted to read his or her story first. Lillian waved her arm in the air, then read, slurping her words, delighted with herself. She wrote about her two-year-old grandson and it was very funny the way she described him. The whole class clapped when she finished. A couple of other people read, then Charles read, slowly and seriously, licking his lips between nearly every word. Again the class clapped.

That applause was like champagne bubbles. I lost my head and raised my hand. The teacher nodded. I read, "My frind Whitney. Shes an ardis. She likes the truth. Her hart wants to be open. But shes afrad other peopels failyer is contajus. Wat she thinks is other peopels failyer. I lid to her. We are no longer frinds."

A rock hard silence.

Then someone murmured, "That's sad."

Someone else said, "That's deep about being an artist."

Charles started to clap. I wanted to elbow him, say, "Stop it!" Other people started clapping. The whole class was clapping. I tried to resist it but I could not stop the applause from getting inside my chest.

When they finished I could feel my mouth stretched open. I was smiling. The teacher said, "Read it again. I'd like to hear that again."

And that was the moment the slow motion ended and normal speed kicked in. I read my story again, louder this time, probably looking every bit as goofily pleased with myself as Lillian. What I liked about my story was that it was true.

At the break I drank instant coffee and ate about twelve Lorna Doones, grinning and chatting with the other new readers as if I had known them for years. Of course, I had. They were my dad. They were me.

20

I SAT AT MY NEW KITCHEN TABLE. It stood smack in the middle of the room—where else could it go?—and was only about two-feet square. I found it, along with a chair, at a garage sale down the street. Though I bought the table, and wanted it, I still resented it a little. Every time I sat down I heard her voice, "Where do you eat? Where do you write?" I didn't quite yet want to admit I liked having a place to eat. Or to write.

Tonight I had *Desert of the Heart* pressed against the wooden grain of the table. Mickey laid curled in a ball on my bed.

"R-a-n-d-o-m," I called out to Mickey.

Quiet animal sounds came from the bed.

"Speak up," I said. "I can't hear you when you mumble."

"Just like it sounds," he shouted. "Random!"

"Thank you. I should have gotten that one," I agreed. I'd been trying to read *Desert of the Heart* for a couple of weeks and was only on page ten.

"Do you think I should go over there?" Mickey whimpered.

"To her *house*?"

"Yeah."

"And do what?"

"I don't know," he moaned. "Talk to her."

"No, I don't think you should do that. What about s-a-r-c-a-s-m?"

"Sarcasm. *You* should know that word."

A sentence later I got stuck again and started to ask Mickey but he said, "I could go over and just explain—"

"Promise me you won't go over to Sheila's house." How could I make Mickey understand that you don't *explain* your way back into someone's life? It doesn't work that way. I closed my book. To distract him, I said, "Listen to this. I went up to Deirdre Felix's house on Tuesday to fix a flat on her bike and—"

"House calls for a flat?" Mickey sat up and rubbed his eyes.

"Yeah, big deal. Anyway, her house was practically empty. 'Where's all the art?' I asked. She said Arnie took it. Can you believe that? The court is giving her the house but the art wasn't mentioned. So he took it. Half the furniture too."

"That's deep," Mickey said, engaged in the conversation for once. Other people's tragedies had become very interesting to him. "But aren't you getting kind of weird about Deirdre Felix?"

"What are you talking about?"

"You got on my case about Sheila being sixteen. Deirdre Felix is what, sixty or sixty-five?"

"It's not like that. It's not a romantic thing."

"If you say so." He curled up into a ball again.

Now he had *my* attention. "What I mean is, it's not a sexual thing. At least I don't think it is. But I do feel kind of in love with her."

Mickey didn't answer.

"Listen, why don't you come riding with us on Saturday? You could meet her. Besides, you haven't been on your bike in weeks."

Mickey groaned.

"Damn it, Mickey. Get off your butt and come riding."

"I'll get off my butt and come riding as soon as you get a new tutor. I'm tired of telling you all those words."

"More deals, huh? I don't think so."

"Then stop lecturing me."

I sighed. "I'm going to bed now."

Mickey slid off my bed and put on his jacket. It hung crooked, not even pulled all the way over one shoulder. His eyes looked like a racoon's.

Even though his interminable sulking drove me crazy, I hated seeing Mickey so miserable. I wished there were a way I could get it into his brain that he would love and be loved again. I wished he were a lot further along on this particular learning curve. I even wished, sometimes, that he had been better socialized as a man.

I put a hand on his chest and pushed. He fell back on the bed like a mannequin, a body with no will. I lifted his legs up and then got a cool washcloth to lay across his brow.

"You want to spend the night?"

He may have nodded. In any case, he didn't move.

I brushed my teeth, took off my jeans and bra, and crawled into bed in my T-shirt. Mickey lay on top of the bedspread with the wash cloth over his eyes.

"Maybe," I said, "maybe we should get to work on our bike shop. You know, look for the space or something."

Mickey snatched the wash cloth off his face. "Really?" he said. "You think so?"

I got the smile I was fishing for, his crazy face unfolding for the first time in days. I rolled over and kissed his cheek. "Maybe. Now go to sleep."

"Flirt with her," I told Mickey. We were having supper at Mel's Diner and Mickey thought the waitress was pretty.

"Yeah right," he said as if she wouldn't be interested in him in a million years.

"Adjust your attitude." I reached across the table and gently punched his chest, hoping to activate that inner fist I had glimpsed. Sometimes it showed. At work he was a little more butch, a little grainier. Sometimes his melted chocolate eyes looked more like old brown bottle glass, the kind you find on the roadside, sharp and reflective. And I knew that was a good thing. Sweet wasn't enough.

The waitress returned and slammed down two glasses of ice water. I kicked Mickey under the table and tried to telepathically send the message, *Flirt now.*

Mickey stared at his menu.

"You ready?" the waitress asked.

"Not yet," I said. As she slid the order pad in her apron pocket, I added, "Actually I'll need a couple extra minutes to read the menu. I'm a new reader." She looked blank, so I said, "You know, I'm just learning to read."

"Oh!" she said, visibly jarred, then very slowly and with exaggerated enunciation, "Well—you—just—take—your—time." After she left Mickey shook his head and said, "Do you have to tell everyone everything?"

"Yes," I said, "I do."

The waitress was the sixth person and still counting, other than Mickey and Deirdre Felix of course, that I'd come out to as a new reader in the past few weeks. Last week my mother said, "Lori, it's always something with you. You have an excuse for everything." Like I had fabricated a disability for attention.

When the waitress returned about a half hour later, I ordered spicy french fries and a turkey burger. She turned to Mickey and asked, "What about you, hon?" Like he was five years old.

Still, when she left, I said, "You didn't even look at her."

"I'm not interested. She's pretty, that's all I said. I don't want anyone else."

I rolled my eyes.

"Don't roll your eyes at me."

"Here she is again," I said. "Just smile your gorgeous smile at her. That's all you have to do."

She put the plate of spicy french fries between us. "I'll be back with your burgers."

"You didn't do it."

Mickey was silent.

"Did I embarrass you by telling her I couldn't read?"

"You always embarrass me."

"Sorry."

He shrugged. "Besides, you're *not* a new reader. You don't have a tutor. All you do is go cycling with your ex-tutor."

I was hurt he didn't count the piles of books in my cottage, the evenings I spend struggling through *Desert of the Heart*, determined to read one whole book, while he lay sulking on my bed. He had a point though. I said, "I'm waiting for her to get through her divorce."

"That could take years."

"How'd you manage to change the topic from you and the waitress to me and reading?"

"I told you. I don't care about the waitress."

"Have some respect," I said. "Her name tag says 'Phyllis.' Don't just call her 'the waitress.'"

Mickey smiled. The waitress returned with our burgers and Mickey winked at her. "Thanks, Phyllis."

I choked on a fry, then laughed so hard I sprayed some of the chewed up potato out of my mouth.

"Stop it," Mickey said. "Now she's looking over here."

Then suddenly Mickey's face looked like he'd just seen a ten-day-old corpse.

I followed the line of his gaze and saw, at the door to Mel's Diner, Sheila with another girl and two boys. "Shit," I said.

The hostess led Sheila and her friends to a table between ours and the door. One of the teenage boys put his hand on Sheila's butt and squeezed. She squealed and slapped his hand away.

"We'll just go," I told Mickey. "We'll just walk out. Come on. Don't even look at her. Just walk with me."

I put my hand between his shoulder blades and gently pushed him toward the door. He cooperated until we got just past Sheila's table. Then he twisted around.

"Why haven't you called me?" he asked her. "You could have at least called. Your parents can't stop you from using the telephone." As if he believed the parents story.

The other girl, an artificial blonde with heavily made-up eyes, opened her mouth into a big O and put her long, pink-nailed fingers over it. Sheila pressed her lips together nervously but her eyes remained opaque and unreadable.

The two guys started laughing.

Mickey and I had eaten here about five times in the last couple of weeks and it just now dawned on me why. Mel's Diner was a teenage hangout. Why hadn't I seen through his recent obsession with hamburgers and french fries?

Mickey worked his way over to Sheila's side of the table with me right behind him. I put my arm around his waist, trying to look like his new lover but fearing that I looked more like his attendant. Still, I sensed that my touch helped.

Then his lip started trembling. Oh god, Mickey was going to cry in front of these adolescents. The two boys were wrenching around in their chairs, elbowing each other, hacking out laughs. Finally one said, "You know this dude, Sheila?"

She looked down at the knife and fork which she clenched in her hands. She didn't laugh along with the others but she wouldn't look at Mickey either.

I thought, Sheila's only sixteen. What does she know about anything?

I was grateful that Mickey didn't cry after all. He took the knife and fork out of Sheila's hands and she let him. "Okay," he said. "Okay."

Together we walked out of Mel's Diner, Mickey still carrying the knife and fork, and I knew that he would never, never ever until the day he died, forget the sound of those kids' laughter.

21

On the first Saturday in October I hung out with the smokers on the sidewalk in front of the library. The program would begin in fifteen minutes and most of the new readers and audience were already inside. Charles and his entire extended family—wife, two daughters, brother, sister-in-law and three nieces—were dressed as if for a wedding. I felt way underdressed and way underprepared. I didn't think I could go through with this event. Spontaneously telling librarians, waitresses and even customers at work that I was a new reader was one thing, but reading my own writing out loud in public—on a microphone—was another. This was supposed to be a celebration for those of us who had completed the writing class but to me it felt like raw exposure. I hadn't invited anyone I knew.

I had begun to wonder if I could just sort of fade away, slip behind the building and disappear down a back street without Charles or anyone else noticing, when the Harley pulled up to the curb. The driver, a large woman wearing Levi's, a black leather jacket and motorcycle boots, helped another large woman wearing support hose and a glossy red party dress climb off the back. The passenger pulled off her helmet and handed it to the driver. The woman in the red dress was Lillian.

"Mom," the other woman said, "what time do you want me to fetch you?"

"Don't worry, baby," Lillian answered. "I'll get a ride."

"Break a leg," the helmeted head said and the Harley roared away, blending into the traffic on University Avenue.

I turned to greet Lillian. "Was that the daughter with the two-year-old grandson you wrote about?" I asked.

Lillian laughed. "Goodness, no. Maria's not married."

A moment later the Harley returned to the curb. This time Maria parked and got off the bike. She opened a saddle bag and took out a red patent leather purse with a gold clasp. I had to smile at the combination of the motorcycle gear and that party purse. She spotted Lillian and then smiled herself. "Mom, I almost rode off with your purse."

"Oh!" Lillian took the purse that matched her dress. "You sure you don't want to stay, baby? They're gonna have good snacks."

"Yeah, I'm sure," Maria said, then she noticed me.

"Nice bike," I said.

"You ride?"

"Well, yeah," I lied. Partially lied.

Maria waved me over to the bike. She pulled off her helmet and set it on the seat, then squatted down to show me some work she'd done on the engine. I admired the hardware and got a good look at Maria too. The woman Lillian called "baby" and tried to tempt with snacks was probably ten years older than me and had short graying hair.

Making conversation, I asked, "Are you a mechanic?"

"I'm out of work right now. That's why I'm living with Mom. But yeah I know a lot about bikes."

I confessed then that I was a bicycle mechanic.

"Cool," she said. Then, "Well." She looked at her bike as if it were a woman with whom she wanted time alone.

I held my ground, grinning. To me that bike looked like escape, like power. I needed escape and felt an enormous vacuum of personal power. I didn't want to desert Charles, Lillian, any of them, but I couldn't do this public reading. Not today.

I put a hand on the worn-smooth black leather seat of the motorcycle, moved my fingers back and forth.

"So, uh," Maria said, "Nice to meet you."

"Think I could have a little ride?" I asked.

Maria took a step back.

"I have to get out of here," I explained, cocking my head toward the library. "I'm supposed to be in the program with your mom, but I can't do it. I just can't."

"Oh," she said, getting it. She looked down toward the bay, then back at me, shrugging. "Why not? Where to?"

"How much time do you have?"

She finally relaxed, smiled, said, "I got all day."

"There's this beach where I once saw a peregrine falcon."

"Let's do it."

"Really? You mean it?"

Maria handed me Lillian's helmet, then swung her bulky leg over the black leather seat of the bike and dropped her substantial buttocks. She turned the key in the ignition and the Harley roared to life. I climbed on, shouted directions and we pulled away from the curb.

I tried to clutch a handful of the back of Maria's jacket but the cowhide was too thick, so I wrapped my arms all the way around her. The jacket was unzipped in front and my hands clasped under her breasts. I put my helmeted head against her back and held on tight.

We rode like that for well over an hour, me on a motorcycle holding a woman I didn't even know. There was a clarity about that motorcycle ride, though, a perfect clarity. Maybe it was the thrill of escape, the way freedom can sometimes make everything look and feel transparent, but it was also Maria herself. I liked the feel of her bulk against my chest, against the insides of my arms and thighs. She felt as familiar as home.

When we got to the coast I directed her to the beach where I'd seen the peregrine falcon. She parked the bike and we got off. She laughed at the way I walked in circles, bull-legged, trying to stretch my legs. She said, "I thought you said you ride."

The fog sat heavily on the headlands and sea. If there were any peregrine falcons diving off the cliffs, I didn't see them. We walked down to the big haystack rock where I'd first met Whitney and I climbed up. "Come on," I called down to Maria who looked vexed by the rock. She climbed anyway, embarrassed, I could tell, by her clumsiness. I nestled into one side of a shallow basin on the top of the rock, leaving room for Maria. Out of breath, she lowered herself into the rock bowl where it was impossible not to roll against me. We lay cradled there for a few minutes, not talking, Maria with her eyes closed and me staring up at the oyster-colored sky.

How much had changed since a year ago when I first met Whitney on this rock. Spontaneous flames seemed possible that day as the hot sun spiked the sea, the sand, her hair. But Whitney was right after all: smoke and mirrors. Not just me though. I lied but I wasn't the only one. The woman I met that day was an artist, a woman with white-hot hair sitting on a big rock by the sea. I broke up with a peach suit. The Whitney I might have loved was on the run. It was as if Whitney and I passed one another on our journeys, hers a retreat and mine a homecoming. I leaned into big Maria and looked up at the flat sky, gray and solid that day, and took comfort.

By now the reading would be over. The cookies and coffee swallowed. The microphone dismantled. The cords rolled up, put away in the closet. Okay, so I was in a bit of a retreat myself, but just for today. I wasn't giving up, just taking a break. Charles would definitely hound me for jumping ship.

"Hey, Maria?"

"Yeah."

"Do you read? I mean, *can* you read?"

"Sure." She sat up, moved so that our bodies were no longer touching and looked out at the place where the sea merged with the fog bank, not far away. I bet she couldn't, at least not much.

"You know what I want most of all?" I asked.

Maria said, "Uh uh."

"I want to give my tutor something as big as she gave me."

Maria stiffened, just a tiny bit, but enough that I knew I'd been right about her and reading.

"Sounds good," she said uncomfortably.

"How about getting something to eat," I said to lighten things up. "Like some ribs."

"Sounds good."

We walked back down the beach to the bike, not talking, tossing rocks into the fog-sea, kicking at the sand.

Riding home through the dusk was magical, like soaring through stardust. I loved the speed and reveled in all the space around me. The thing was, Mickey was wrong. I *was* a new reader. I didn't have a tutor, he was right about that, and I needed one, but I knew that language was space, a kind of movement through space, and knowing that made me a reader. I'd get a tutor soon, or maybe Deirdre Felix would soon be ready to start again, but for now I wanted to enjoy all this space, both around and inside me. I remembered those times working with Deirdre Felix when I felt like my insides were getting carved out, then later, those months of feeling empty, like I'd demolished everything I had in me. But I hadn't. I'd only demolished the huge debris of defenses I'd built up around my feelings of inadequacy, of ignorance, of feeling like I had no right. Once I cleared that out, something else could grow in there. Was growing in there. I was never going to go to law school but that wasn't the point. The point was, I was learning to read. And I wanted so badly for someone else to know that. I wanted Deirdre Felix to know that.

We forgot about the ribs, didn't stop for anything, not even gas. I couldn't see the speedometer but it felt like we were going a hundred miles an hour. I wanted to take off my helmet, feel the wind in my hair. I wanted to stand on the black leather seat, stretch out my arms, throw back my head, ride the motorcycle like a trick horsewoman in a circus.

Maria dropped me off late, well after dark. I felt as if I'd been flushed clean, leaving my insides bright and pepperminty. After thanking her for the ride I walked up the dark path to my cottage.

I heard someone coming toward me.

"Lori?"

"Who's that?"

"Me, Edith."

We met on the path and clumped together in a bear hug.

"Oh, I'm sorry for being out of touch for so long, Lori. And oh, I can hardly even say it, that date in May? I feel like such a crumb for totally standing you up."

The May fifth date! The one I thought *I* had been the no-show for. "It's okay," I said, then asked, "Did you break up with—" What was her name? "—your lover?"

"How did you know?" Edith sounded astonished.

"I'm psychic. Come on in. I'll make you supper."

22

I HATED ADMITTING there was a machine I couldn't fix but I had pretty well demolished my tape player last June—the morning after that marathon session of listening to all my tapes, including the one of making love with Whitney—when I stabbed it with a rusty pair of hedging sheers my landlady left out on one of the Adirondack chairs. It was a cheap tape player anyway.

So on my lunch hour on Friday, I ran down to Radio Shack and bought a new deluxe model. That night I talked into it for a long, long time. I told myself about Whitney leaving, her note and my notes. I told myself all about my landlady's rooftop, the police and the night I found Deirdre Felix's hybrid two-wheeler. I talked about my long bike rides and the "marvelous details" I had noticed in the hills, on the coast, in the city streets. Of course I carried on at great length about Deirdre Felix, her art and divorce, our Saturday mornings. I finished up by telling Mickey's story, beginning to end. I had a whole damn book on tape by the time I finished at midnight.

Then I called Mickey. "Eight o'clock tomorrow morning, at the Breezeway Market."

"I was asleep."

"Good. Then you'll be nice and fresh in the morning."

"Okay," he said.

I was stunned. I had called him every Friday night for several weeks. Sometimes he snarled no, sometimes he whined no, but it was always no.

"What?" I said, wanting to hear that word again, that one word that meant change, that admitted to a future.

"Okay," he said again and hung up on me.

"Love you too." I kissed the phone and before going to bed, turned on my tape player to report this progress on the Mickey front.

I overslept.

At eight fifteen, as I stood straddling my bike waiting for the light to change so I could cross over to the Breezeway Market, I watched Mickey and Deirdre Felix sitting together on the bench next to the espresso vendor. Steam swirled out of the matching cups they held and I wondered who had bought. Mickey sat with his legs spread, gesturing with his hands, telling a story in his highly entertaining way, clearly at ease with Deirdre Felix. He stood up to tell a dramatic part and at this distance, I noticed a change in Mickey I hadn't seen up close. The only words I could put to it were: no longer a virgin. He looked sexy in his jersey covered with bicycle company logos and his black tights. He still moved in that characteristically goofy way, dramatic and silly and sweet all at once, very Mickey, but rather than seeming to be saddled with that particular style, now he owned it.

By the time I got through the traffic signal and joined them, I'd become jealous of their apparent chumminess.

"So you've already introduced yourselves?" I asked.

"Yes." Deirdre Felix glanced at her watch. She too wore black

189

cycling tights and a bright blue cycling jersey. "Miguel and I have been chatting for a while."

"I'm late," I said. "I'm sorry."

Mickey was as neurotic as she was about punctuality, so I guessed they had already bonded around timeliness.

"Sorry," I said again, then to Mickey I added, "Miguel, huh?"

"Miguel was telling me about your bike shop," Deirdre Felix said, politely catching me up on their conversation.

"Oh," I said, thinking she meant the one we worked in, but one glimpse of Mickey's sheepish look told me otherwise. He had told her about the fantasy bike shop.

"It's so exciting," Deirdre Felix enthused.

I fired Mickey a furious look.

He recovered from sheepishness quickly and announced, "Yeah, I told Deirdre maybe we could hire her."

"Ex*cuse* me?"

"I wouldn't mind a job," Deirdre Felix said. "I may need a job."

There was no bike shop. What was Mickey doing?

"The thing is," Mickey said, speaking directly to me now, "I may have found a space for the shop. On University Avenue."

I experienced a small psychic earthquake. All the pieces of my world shook hard for a brief moment, broke into segments, then fell into place again.

"Really?" was all I could manage.

Mickey nodded vigorously. "Come on, pumpkin." He put his cold hands on my cheeks, weaving his fingers through the straps of my bike helmet. "Don't be such a chickenshit." He gave my face an energetic shake and I laughed.

"Okay, okay! Can we talk about it later?" I begged.

"Have you noticed," Mickey asked Deirdre Felix, "how tough she always tries to act but how really she's a marshmallow underneath? A chickenshit marshmallow?"

I didn't dare look at Deirdre Felix to see how she responded.

"Let's ride," I said. Enough out of you, Mickey. Already I missed his sulking.

190

"Are we gonna do Grizzly Peak?" Mickey asked. He and I usually rode up Grizzly Peak for starters but I didn't think Deirdre Felix was ready for that much hill-climbing.

As I started to object, I saw her glance at the hills and say nothing. If she didn't object, why should I? So I said, "We should go up Tunnel Road," which is the most gradual ascent.

We didn't talk as we negotiated the city streets. When we arrived at the beginning of Tunnel Road, we settled into a slow pace. The morning was bright and clear.

After the first mile of climbing, Mickey said, "I don't know why I never brought Sheila up here."

"Would she have liked it?" Deirdre Felix asked.

"She loved nature." Mickey spoke as if she were dead.

"You don't see her anymore?"

Mickey launched into his history with Sheila, a catalogue of her virtues, and placed all the blame of her disappearance on her father, in spite of the scene in Mel's Diner, which he did not relate to Deirdre Felix.

At first I felt jealous of the instant and easy intimacy that Mickey obviously felt with Deirdre Felix, compared to my own intimacy with her which felt hard-won and formal. But when I turned and looked at her riding directly behind me, she smiled and winked. I could tell that Mickey delighted her and that she also found his steely innocence, his unwavering earnestness, comical. Not in a mean way. I knew what she meant. What a great distance there was between their two experiences of love. What a long road it must seem to Deirdre Felix back to Mickey's place.

We stopped often so Deirdre Felix could catch her breath but finally made it to the top of Skyline Boulevard, above Tunnel Road, where we turned left onto the flat part of Grizzly Peak Road. We were still a good mile or two from the top. I pulled off onto the gravel beside the road. There we had a glittering view of the San Francisco Bay and city. Hundreds of sailboats made a rainbow of color in the water.

Breathing hard, Deirdre Felix wheeled her bike up next to

Mickey and put an arm around his shoulder. "I'm sorry about Sheila," she said. Then some laughter escaped her. I could tell she was embarrassed yet couldn't help herself. It was that pressure valve kind of laughter, the all-emotions-rolled-into-one hysterical laughter. Deirdre Felix did it a lot lately, and the way I looked at it, laughing was a pretty good way to release tension, even if it was inappropriate at times.

But Mickey looked hurt.

So to save Deirdre Felix from further embarrassment and to give us all something to laugh about, I said, "Tell him about the grilled mahi mahi."

She burst out laughing. When she recovered, she told the story and Mickey cracked up too. He always loved a good story.

"I guess all three of us are in the same boat," he said.

"Which boat is that?" I asked.

"The broken heart boat."

"Broken heart?" I said at the same time as Deirdre Felix said, "All three?"

I frowned at Mickey.

"What," Mickey said, "you didn't tell her about Whitney?"

"Who's Whitney?" Deirdre Felix asked.

I looked out at the brilliance of the bay again. I wouldn't call what I had about Whitney a broken heart, but why split hairs? Mickey and Deirdre Felix were waiting.

"Remember that sex workshop I told you about?"

The corners of Deirdre Felix's lips twitched again.

I smiled. "You can laugh. It was ridiculous. But I did meet someone there. I think I told you about the woman on the big rock at the beach. Didn't I? Well we got involved."

"And?"

"I guess you could say I fell for her. Sort of."

"I guess you could say that," Mickey mimicked. "*Sort of.* What's with the withholding? Geez, Lori, give it up. I can't believe you didn't tell Deirdre about this."

I fired him another warning look. First of all, how dare he call her by her first name alone. Second of all, I didn't tell her about the ordinary details of my life. Deirdre Felix and I, we read literature and went to the ballet. And now, now I was her coach.

Deirdre Felix folded her arms across her chest. A harsh autumn light, almost a metallic gold, bounced off the bay far below us, and I realized I'd known her for a whole year.

"Cough it up," she said, elbowing Mickey. "Here you are letting us display all our dirty laundry and you're acting all high and mighty."

"Me high and mighty?" I had to laugh at that. "Hardly. It's pretty simple, really. I didn't tell her I couldn't read. I sort of did a lot of lying to cover up. So when she found out, she was mad. Real mad. And she dumped me."

I looked at Mickey who hadn't heard this version before. He lowered his long lashes for a second, then looked at me full square on. He said, "I didn't know that. I didn't know that's what happened."

Deirdre Felix was silent and I didn't want to look at her. I knew she didn't have a whole lot of sympathy for lying and who could blame her?

"She couldn't have handled it even if you had told her," Mickey rallied. "She was too much into her little Oberlin snobbery."

"Oberlin?" Deirdre Felix finally spoke. "Arnie and I met at Oberlin."

"Whoops," Mickey said.

"*Pfft.*" She dismissed Oberlin, then, "So how long were you and Whitney together?"

"Six months."

"How'd she find out?"

So I told Deirdre Felix and Mickey about the BONG meeting and as I got going, I couldn't help putting a funny spin on the story and had them both laughing by the time I got to the part that wasn't so funny, the part in the car where I told Whitney the truth. Everybody's laughter wilted.

I did get two more smiles when I related how Whitney tried

to dump me with a note.

At the end I said, "So you think I deserved it, huh? This hustler took things a few steps too far?"

Deirdre Felix looked tired, like my story had worn her out. She shook her head. "Deserved it? Of course not. You have too big a heart to deserve that kind of pain."

She scooted her bike over to where I straddled mine and gave me a one-armed hug. I felt so shaky and off-center from my confession and her warm words that I lost balance. As she leaned into me, I inclined away. "Whoa!" I yelled, going down. Deirdre Felix, still straddling her own bike, crashed on top of me. "*Ugghh*," I groaned as the teeth on her freewheel dug into the flesh of my leg. The pain was intense and sharp but Deirdre Felix had her head on my shoulder and was laughing so hard her whole body was heaving. The pain, the relief, the warmth of her body all melded together into one big feeling.

"Aren't we a pair!" she cried as Mickey tried to pull her off of me.

Finally untangled and back on our feet, I asked, "Are you okay?"

"Sure. Since I've been riding my bike so much, I've begun to feel rather indestructible." She cocked her arm and made a muscle, smiling at me. "Biking is the best thing that's happened to me in a long time."

Overcompensating for a welling up of tenderness, I growled, "Ready to turn back?"

"Are we at the top?" she wanted to know.

"No but. . . ." After this flat part there was one more good steep stretch to the top of Grizzly Peak.

"Then let's go to the top. Unless you're impatient with all my stops."

"I'm not impatient," I said more forcefully than I intended. "I've got endurance for days."

She smiled at my using that word, endurance, the one I had stumbled over so many times in my reading. She said, "So Miguel has kissed a girl and you're learning to read. That was the deal, wasn't it?"

I looked up at the sun blinking through the canopy of leaves over the road. So she knew. She knew that in spite of all my missed words and bad comprehension, in spite of my tutorless months, I really was learning to read. I thought I was the only one who knew that.

Then she said softly, "How are you going to celebrate?"

My voice came out real gruff. "By getting you to the top of Grizzly Peak on your bike, that's how. Let's go."

I took off, ignoring the sticky blood gluing my tights to my thigh, ignoring the waves of pain emanating from the wound. I rode hard and fast, leaving Deirdre Felix and Mickey behind, just for a moment, because I wanted to feel more than the separate parts of pedal, wind and muscle: I wanted to feel the whole ride. There was a red cliff on my right but to the west the world suddenly felt like a very big place, unfurling into an enormous collage of sky, water and light. I pedaled furiously, gulping in the air, as if all that space were mine to fill.

ABOUT THE AUTHOR

Lucy Jane Bledsoe is the author of *Sweat: Stories and a Novella* (Seal Press, 1995), which was a Lambda Literary Award Finalist, and of two novels for young people, *The Big Bike Race* (Holiday House, 1995) and *Tracks in the Snow* (Holiday House, 1997). Her stories have been published in *New York Newsday, Fiction International, Sister and Brother, Women on Women 2, Women on Women 3, Northwest Literary Forum, Girlfriends, Room of One's Own, Another Wilderness* (Seal Press, 1994) and *Solo* (Seal Press, 1996). She has been awarded a PEN Syndicated Fiction Award, a National Endowment for the Humanities Youthgrant and a Barbara Deming Memorial Money for Women grant. She recently completed a script and story-writing project for the George Lucas Education Foundation in Marin. She writes textbooks and fiction for educational publishers and teaches writing workshops in Bay Area adult literacy programs. She is the editor of several anthologies, including *Heatwave* (Alyson, 1995), *Goddesses We Ain't: Tenderloin Women Writers* (Freedom Voices, 1992) and three collections of writings by newly literate adults.

SELECTED LESBIAN TITLES FROM SEAL PRESS

SWEAT: *Stories and a Novella,* by Lucy Jane Bledsoe. $10.95, 1-878067-64-8. The elusive sanctity of sport. The exquisite rewards of risk. The adventure that is contemporary lesbian life. These are the themes that resonate in this refreshing first collection by Lucy Jane Bledsoe.

THE ME IN THE MIRROR by Connie Panzarino. $12.95, 1-878067-45-1. The memoir of writer, lesbian and disability rights activist and artist Connie Panzarino, who has been living with a rare muscular disease since birth.

ALMA ROSE by Edith Forbes. $10.95, 1-878067-33-8. A brilliant lesbian novel filled with unforgettable characters and the vibrant spirit of the West.

OUT OF TIME by Paula Martinac. $9.95, 0-931188-91-1. A delightful and thoughtful novel about lesbian history and the power of memory. *Winner of the 1990 Lambda Literary Award for Best Lesbian Fiction.*

HOME MOVIES by Paula Martinac. $10.95, 1-878067-32-X. This timely story charts the emotional terrain of losing a loved one to AIDS and the intricacies of personal and family relationships.

MARGINS by Terri de la Peña. $10.95, 1-878067-19-2. An insightful story about family relationships, recovery from loss, creativity and lesbian passion.

LATIN SATINS by Terri de la Peña. $10.95, 1-878067-52-4. This second novel by the prize-winning author tells the lives and loves of a group of young Chicana singers.

LOVERS' CHOICE by Becky Birtha. $10.95, 1-878067-41-9. Provocative stories charting the course of women's lives by an important Black lesbian feminist writer.

CEREMONIES OF THE HEART: *Celebrating Lesbian Unions,* second edition, edited by Becky Butler. $16.95, 1-878067-87-7. An anthology of twenty-five personal accounts of ceremonies of commitment, from the momentous decision to the day of celebration.

LESBIAN COUPLES: *Creating Healthy Relationships for the 90s* by D. Merilee Clunis and G. Dorsey Green. $12.95, 1-878067-37-0. The first definitive guide for lesbians that describes the pleasures and challenges of being part of a couple. Also available on audiocassette, $9.95, 0-931188-85-7.

THE LESBIAN PARENTING BOOK: *A Guide to Creating Families and Raising Children* by D. Merilee Clunis and G. Dorsey Green. $16.95, 1-878067-68-0. This practical and readable book, filled with humor and wisdom, covers a wide range of parenting topics as well as issues specifically relevant to lesbian families. Information on each child development stage is also provided.

GAUDÍ AFTERNOON by Barbara Wilson. $9.95, 0-931188-89-X. Amidst the dream-like architecture of Barcelona, this high-spirited comic thriller introduces amateur sleuth Cassandra Reilly as she chases people of all genders and motives. *Winner of the 1990 Lambda Literary Award for Best Lesbian Mystery and the British Crime Writers Association's 92 Award.*

THE DYKE AND THE DYBBUK by Ellen Galford. $10.95, 1-878067-51-6. A fun, feisty, feminist romp through Jewish folklore as an ancient spirit returns to haunt a modern-day London lesbian.

GIRLS, VISIONS AND EVERYTHING by Sarah Schulman. $9.95, 0-931188-38-5. A spirited romp through Manhattan's Lower East Side featuring lesbian-at-large Lila Futuransky. By the author of *After Delores, Empathy* and *Rat Bohemia.*

ORDERING INFORMATION

Individuals: If you are unable to obtain a Seal Press title from a bookstore, please order from us directly. Enclose payment with your order and 16.5% of the book total for shipping and handling. Washington residents should add 8.2% sales tax. Checks, MasterCard and Visa accepted. If ordering with a credit card, don't forget to include your name as it appears on the card, the expiration date and your signature.

Orders Dept.
Seal Press
3131 Western Avenue, Suite 410, Seattle, Washington 98121
1-800-754-0271 orders only; (206) 283-7844 / (206) 285-9410 fax
sealprss@scn.org

Visit our website at http://www.sealpress.com